THE
CROW
BOX

NIKKI RAE

Nikki Rae
THE CROW BOX
The Shadow & Ink Series, book one
Illustrations by the author.

Book design by Inkstain Interior Book Designing

"On a dark, dark night

In a dark, dark wood

In a dark, dark house

In a dark, dark room

In a dark, dark cupboard

On a dark, dark shelf

In a dark, dark box

There was a ghost."

—A HALLOWEEN FOLKTALE

PART ONE:
WHITE NOISE

CHAPTER
ONE

IT STARTED WITH A VOICE.

The same one you hear in the dark, when you're under the covers ready to fall asleep—not quite awake, but not dreaming either. That place where your mind wanders and whispers secrets that will be forgotten by the morning. You convince yourself that it isn't all that important anyway by the time the sun rises.

Only that voice never called me by name. I never felt as though my mind needed to repeat it like a secret prayer told in the dark corners of a mausoleum. A poem written in fresh, black ink only to be closed in its notebook and locked away in a drawer.

Corbin, it said. I brought the blankets closer to my chin as I rolled over, convinced I was just hearing things. The house was settling, the TV was on in the next room, and wind was blowing past the windows in warning of an imminent storm. Everyone in the house was asleep. I was just over tired and my thoughts were running away from me as my brain tried to grasp onto the concept of rest.

Corbin.

"Whisper" wasn't the word. It was as if feathers had fallen from the sky and gently landed around me, grazing my skin as I finally opened my eyes and stared at the ceiling. My eyes travelled over the pink canopy that I was too old for, the matching satin comforter and pillows making slick sounds as I settled against them in my new position on my back. I was never really afraid of the dark, but Mom kept wall lights in every room of the house. Mine was no exception. I usually unplugged it before I went to bed; the dim glow was enough to distract me from falling asleep, but sometimes I was simply too tired to remember to turn it off.

There was no one in the room with me and I could see through the crack under my door that there was no light from outside. No soft blue glow that told me the TV was on in the next room where Mom had fallen asleep on the couch. In this small space between two and three in the morning, I was completely alone.

I closed my eyes again. I had my critiques in the morning and so much of my grade depended on whether I could make my professors believe there was deeper symbolism in my self-portraits than I ever had the energy to produce.

I took a deep breath, deciding I was just nervous about the end of the semester and my mind was making things up to fixate on.

Concentrating on the sound of my own breathing, I folded my hands across my stomach and listened. No other sounds. Just me. As my inhales turned to low white noise and my exhales became a plain, even backdrop for unborn dreams to dance on, my thoughts began to inevitably drift once more, like they were in a tiny boat on a vast sea of black water.

There was a dark green cloud on the canvas of my eyelids and it morphed into different shapes I didn't recognize, colors I did recognize, but then forgot. Something with fur turned into something with fins, and then the creature had wings and flapped them fluidly a few times as I rolled onto my side again, my head sinking into the cool pillow.

The sound was the soft texture of two fingers rubbing together in the dark. It didn't wake me this time; only seemed to send me deeper into sleep. I was glad.

Corbin, it said without saying. It was a language I wished I could grasp, but it was too heavy. It made my eyelids close tighter, my limbs that much more weighted.

The image of the winged creature was nothing more than a colorful shadow, an impression left behind my eyes as if I had just come in from outside on a sunny day. It changed slightly. Now the wings were more defined. So much that they were all I saw for a long time.

Then a head formed. There was something decidedly human about it, but I couldn't see a face. Only shadows.

As soon as I recognized the shapes, they dispersed and contorted, flattened and then turned dark, like there was nothing there at all.

Do you like my form?

It was the sound of waves kissing the shore. Loud and over-powering, but soothing, sending me farther over the edge of sleep. A step closer to dreams and darkness; rest.

I felt myself sigh under the warm blankets, the pink satin from my childhood swallowing me up. *Corbin?* This time, a question. Or was that another sigh? Was I snoring?

It didn't matter. It would all look different by morning.

LIGHT. BIRDS CHIRPING. THE SOUND of green leaves brushing past one another in a slight breeze as a car passed down the street. Drawers were being opened and dishes clattered against the table. Mom was awake, cooking something that smelled mostly burnt.

I rolled over, rubbing the sleep from my eyes and realized I had slept in my makeup again when my hands came away smudged in black. I slipped out of bed and stretched, turning off the nightlight by the door.

The nightlight.

Was there a voice?

I blinked a few times as I stared at the small bulb. No, I didn't hear voices. I was just tired.

Inching down the hall and into the bathroom, I showered and brushed my teeth. In the mirror, I got rid of the make up the water hadn't taken care of, my grey eyes turning red. Then I thoroughly combed my black hair out of my face and behind my ears. I hated how I looked wet—like some horror movie character. The dark circles under my eyes didn't help. It was Thursday. One class left and I would be free.

I took comfort in that as I did my makeup and dressed in jeans and a plain black tank. The bathroom and my room were probably the cleanest in the entire house. Mom had a habit of collecting things, gathering them around her like they added up to a life well spent. She came home at least once a week with something new. "Antique" newspapers that sat in piles on the floor. Books that were so water damaged you couldn't read any of the words anymore. There was the teacup collection in the china cabinet in the living room. Mom didn't drink tea.

And there were the couches. Mom loved furniture; couches were her favorite. In our small living room, she had somehow fit two sofas, two armchairs, and a loveseat. We could only sit on one of them; the rest were homes for more lost-and-found objects.

In order to get from the bathroom to the living room and into the kitchen, I had to maneuver around all of this and more in the small path we had worn down in the rooms like experienced hikers on a familiar trail.

"You awake, sweetie?" I heard Mom call from the kitchen. The closer I got, the more intense the smell of burnt food became.

I found her over the stove, cooking something on the rusted range. If the living room was cluttered, the kitchen was a disaster area. It wasn't that Mom wasn't clean. She was one of the cleanest people I knew; wiping down counter space that showed, mopping the visible floor, dusting every knickknack we owned at least once a week. She was just unorganized. And a pack rat. And a little crazy.

"Burnt toast?" I asked as I tried to step around a stack of

expired coupons Mom had refused to throw out, convinced she could still use them three months past their expiration.

Mom half-turned in her fuzzy yellow bathrobe. She had curlers in her hair and makeup on already. It was a good day for her. She usually didn't get dressed at all, sticking to pajamas and bed-tossed hair. "Bagel," she said, smiling. "At least I still know how to make eggs." She grabbed a chipped plate from the cupboard.

I cleared a small space on the table for us, pushing a pile of coupons, winter clothes, and even a few stuffed animals to one side. I did the same for two chairs, taking the stacks of paper off and adding them to the mountain of things on the other end.

"Here you go, sweetie," Mom said as she set a plate of steaming eggs in front of me. "Scrambled. You need a full stomach to pass your finals."

"Thanks, Mom," I said, looking up at her and smiling. I knew there would be shells in the eggs. I knew they would be runny in the center with too much salt, but Mom only tried doing things like this when she was feeling good and those times were hard to come by.

Mom sat down next to me and took her morning meds with half a glass of orange juice. I took an aspirin in preparation for my day ahead.

"Got anything fun planned for today?" I asked.

Mom smiled. "You know," she said, taking a forkful of eggs. "I was thinking about hitting some garage sales and getting out and gardening for a little while."

I chewed my eggs twice before swallowing, too afraid of what my teeth would come into contact with if I broke it up any more than that. "That's good, Mom," I said. "It's good to get outside."

"It is, isn't it?" she said enthusiastically. "I really think the sun does wonders for me."

I drank my orange juice, taking my plate and placing it in the sink. I set to work cleaning up the pan and stove as Mom ate the rest of her food. She hadn't had a job in over six months, but she couldn't work in her condition. Her doctors had deemed her too sick to work and most days I was unsure of whether their decision to put her on disability had helped her mental health or made it worse. Instead of being forced out of bed by a job and having to be a certain place by a certain time every day, she stayed indoors, sometimes not even bothering to turn on the lights. When she wasn't in bed, she was wandering around trying to organize things but refusing to throw away any of it. She would spend hours pushing one pile around the room, moving a solitary object from shelf to shelf before becoming frustrated and giving up.

"I'm out," I said. "Got to get those grades." I leaned over her chair and kissed her on the cheek.

"Good luck, Corbin," she said as she cleared her own plate. "You're talented, sweetie. I know you'll do well."

Yes, Corbin. The voice again. I was halfway down the hall, on my way back to my room when I turned.

"Did you say something?" I asked.

Mom smiled. "I said good luck."

I blinked a few times, my skin hot. I turned back around as

a breeze ran through the house. Mom had opened most of the windows.

My portfolio sat leaning against the wall; I had left my paints sitting on my desk overnight, too tired after finishing my final before crawling into bed. I couldn't be bothered to clean it up and pack it all away. Gathering the various tubes and brushes, I put them back into my converted toolbox.

I folded up the newspaper I had laid down so I didn't mess up the wood of my desk and crumpled it up, disposing of it in my small garbage can in the corner. I couldn't stand knowing I would come home to a messy room. I needed to make it clean again before I left.

As I was getting rid of the last few pages of repurposed coupon pages Mom wouldn't notice I had taken, something caught my eye. At first, it only seemed to be a glob of green paint, but then as I looked closer, I noticed that it had a distinct shape. Two dark wings in perfect symmetry. While they appeared to be those of a bird, the body was more like a dragon fly. I must have doodled it when I got bored of my five millionth self-portrait the night before. I could use it for a painting. Tearing out the small blob, I tacked it to my bulletin board for future reference.

I felt my hair being lifted from my shoulder and turned, expecting Mom to be there wishing me good luck again, but there was nothing there but my open window, a breeze flowing through so strongly that it ruffled the fabric of my shirt and gave me goose bumps despite the hot day outside.

CHAPTER
TWO

I CAME HOME WITH MY C+ for my Basic Drawing assignment clutched tightly in my hand in the form of a "critique" paper my professor had deemed necessary. Comments included. I was fine with it; it wasn't like I tried for something higher. I took a few steps into the living room before I decided to just sit in the swing on the porch. With its jungle of miscellaneous plants and flowers, it was just as crowded as the inside of the house, but at least I wouldn't trip over anything.

A slight breeze blew my dark hair into my face as I reached into my portfolio for my real sketchbook. The one I kept for the things that came to me in sleep or when I was trying to keep my mind occupied and not fall asleep in class. I wanted to recreate the green blob on the newspaper, so I started sketching it out with a pencil, the soft scratching sounds taking away the stress of the past few days. I could concentrate on nothing but that sound for hours—lead against paper, the skin of my fingers against the sketch pad. The sun was dimmer now than it was this morning; a few clouds rolled in, but there was still enough light to see.

The wings were definitely the hardest part. Symmetry wasn't my strongest skill. If I spent hours trying to get it right, sometimes it worked out fine, but mostly, I ended up getting frustrated and turned the thing into something else. Hair would cover an eye. A hand would be holding something when the other sat perfectly on a naked, lifelike hip. I wondered how I had gotten the wings so perfect the night before. Maybe it was something I just couldn't duplicate.

I settled on concentrating on the dragonfly, abandoning the wings for the time being. I made a small line where the tail began, hooking through a delicate curve. Without finishing the rest of its body, I started on the eyes. I thought they would look better the bigger they were, so I could play with the details of them. Two large orbs stared back at me, bringing the half-creature, half-dream to life.

I was just about to dive back into the wings when Mom pulled up in the driveway, the sound of gravel crunching under the wheels of her beat-up red Mercury. She rolled down the window and called out to me. "Hey, honey! Home so soon?"

It was four thirty. Mom had most likely been out shopping since I left this morning. We would have to make space in the house once again. Things would need to be moved, piles of stuff would touch the ceiling sooner than we realized.

"I passed," I said, coming to the driver's side and waiting for her to climb out.

Mom had since taken the rollers out of her dark brown hair and it hung in neatly tamed waves around her face. She had even put a little red lipstick on and was wearing a blue dress with cheery flowers painted on it. She looked good. The best she had in weeks. Maybe the new combination of medicine was finally working for her. Maybe she would be happy from now on. Waiting for her drugs to kick in and stabilize was like stepping onto a field full of eggs and praying you didn't crack any.

"Well," she said. "It looks like we should celebrate, then."

I was surprised when Mom only held a small shopping bag in her hands. Usually when she went out all day, she came back with the entire car filled with items. She handed me the translucent brown plastic. "I would have wrapped it, but you're home early."

Again, I wasn't. She was home late. It didn't matter.

"This is for me?" I asked. Mom had learned from me at a young age that I didn't like it when she got me presents. Most of the time her presents ended up in the closet or somewhere else in the house. I had no use for antique dolls or dressers that had more drawers than I had clothes to fill.

"Of course," she said as she followed me back inside the house. The place I had cleared off for us to eat this morning was already filled in with stuff once again, like the house itself was some kind of viscous material; if my presence poked a hole in something, I only had to leave for a few hours and it would fill in the blank spaces. Mom and I sat down on the one empty couch in the living room. She played with my hair as I set the heavy bag on my lap. "Well, open it," she said. "I want to know what you think."

Reaching blindly into the bag, my hand was met with a cold, hard surface. It was smooth, and it was small enough that I could lift it with one hand.

Setting the empty bag on the floor where it would most likely be forgotten if I didn't throw it away, I set the object on my lap. It was about the size of a paperback novel, yet it was thick, made out of a dark oak wood. It was a box with a small drawer and latch. The latch was covered in what looked like deep red candle wax, and around the edges was intricate metalwork that had most likely at one time been silver, but now most of it had rusted black. Small flecks of it came off on my fingers and a hollow clunking sound came when I shook it.

"I know," Mom said. "It's a little beat up, but I figured you could clean it up and put some supplies in it."

I smiled a little at Mom's eager face. "Thanks," I said.

"You hate it."

I stared down at the box in my hands. Placing my fingers around the small metal knob of the drawer, I gave it a gentle tug. The inside was lined with faded red velvet. I tried opening the lid, but the wax prevented that.

"Yeah," Mom said, noticing. "I think someone might have hidden something in there. I shook it, and it sounds empty, but you never know."

It did look like it was once some sort of jewelry box. I shook it tentatively. No sound.

"You hate it," she repeated.

"No," I told her quickly. "It's just...different."

Mom placed a finger on the box. "I know it sounds crazy," she said, emphasizing the word that she hated. "But I saw this at a garage sale and just really thought you'd love it."

I slid the drawer back in. The sound reminded me a lot of paper and pencil working together to bring a drawing to life.

"I do love it," I said, smiling for Mom. "Thanks."

She smiled widely then, showing the one chipped canine tooth on the left side. It was tiny, but I always managed to notice it when it made an appearance. Maybe because it was so rare to see it. "Congratulations, sweetie," she said. "Do you want some lemonade?" she called from inside the kitchen, not bothering to turn on any lights.

"No thanks," I called back, snapping the sketchpad shut and resting my present on my lap. The velvet was musty—like it had been pickled in an attic filled with exposed insulation and yellowing photo albums. "I'm meeting Jordan."

Mom reappeared at the door, leaning her hand against the frame. "Let me put that inside then," she suggested, holding out her hand.

I stared down at my lap, sliding the drawer open and closed. "Can you put it on my desk for me?" I asked. "Any spot that's clear is fine."

"Sure." She smiled, her palm held out expectantly.

I gave her the box, fully aware of the weight of it, and then I noticed the sudden nothingness as it left me.

"OKAY," JORDAN SAID, LIFTING MY chin the slightest bit. "Just like that. That's perfect."

We were in her room at her parents' house. She had more or less built the thing herself, turning a small space of the garage into a room with wood and insulation. She had a bed built into the wall that she made to look like a cave. You had to crawl through a door to get to it. As a couch, she had the backseat of a car that was repurposed, an afghan her mother owned as a teenager in the seventies thrown over it. She never used any light brighter than 25 watts, and she had red lampshades that cast the room in a soft glow. I sat on a stool in the middle of the room as Jordan took her place behind her easel. We had been modeling for each other since we met over three years ago, so I was comfortable being naked in front of her as she sketched. I was just grateful she hadn't made me hold a ridiculous prop or sit with a bowl of fruit on my head.

"How long you want me to hold these poses?" I asked.

She tucked a strand of her black-and-white striped hair behind her ear, not even glancing at me as she set the timer on her phone. "Ten minutes each?" she asked, although we both knew she wasn't giving me an option.

"Okay."

I sat with my arms at my sides, palms face up in my lap, staring slightly to the left. I knew that I was merely the form, the wirework for the finished product. She needed me to build off of to make a real image. I wasn't anything special with my nose that was too long, my lips that were too full, the small smattering of freckles across my nose and my long straight black hair that she had me drape over one shoulder, but in her painting, I could be a queen with an enemy's head in my lap, a skeleton with butterflies bursting from my chest. I was just the first draft. By the time she was done, no one would even guess what was underneath.

Music floated from the hidden speakers around her room, the voice of some melancholy girl singing in a deep voice set to a lone guitar. I usually fell asleep when she played this stuff, but I was wide awake today. Jordan took a sip of her white wine from her mug and went off into her world, only glancing at me now and then to get the proportions right. We often modeled for each other because we each knew what the other wanted. She always asked for a simple pose and I always wanted something a little more complicated, but we knew each others' rhythms. We could talk to each other or be quiet and be fine with either. Jordan was the only other person I knew that was as serious about art as I was. Most people used it as an excuse to get out of "real" classes like Math and English—like color theory and two-point perspective were easy A's.

I stared across the room, picking a spot behind Jordan's head where she had hung a large blue lobster sculpture she made in high school ceramics. She had since added a Santa hat and the crustacean was also holding a fake bouquet of roses. I focused on the petals, letting my mind drift as the dark red became darker, the rest of the room fading away.

I let the music become white noise that lulled me into the

space between being awake and unaware of the room around me. Jordan's dim red lights faded into dark grey. Her Christmas lights draped over a stolen mannequin (which she had named Erica) from a Macy's dumpster twinkled in the background behind her, behind the large easel she sat behind, her face covered by it except when she peered around the edge to glance at one of my features or another. I was never sure what it was about these afternoons together that always made me feel complete. Making art. Being part of it. Being formed from paint and color when my life was more or less a wash of grey and brown. My mind shut off. My limbs were light. Anything could happen in the space between the first line being drawn and the piece being completed, brought to life.

"Corbin."

I thought it was the voice, but when I blinked, Jordan was waving a hand from behind the canvas, staring at me. She sounded like she had said my name more than once already.

"What?"

She laughed to herself. "I *said* how'd your finals go?"

Keeping my expression as still as I could, I said, "Eh, they were critiques. Someone's the kiss-ass, someone's the defensive baby, someone vows to quit school. Same ole, same ole."

She snorted as she cleaned a brush before placing it in her hair for safe keeping. She picked up a smaller, more detailed brush. "Please tell me you weren't one of those."

"Nah," I said. "I just took my C's and left."

"C's," she said like they were the highest grades I could get.

"What did you submit?"

"Oh—" The phone went off; time was up.

I stretched my arms over my head, unconcerned about my exposed flesh, my small breasts shifting with the movement. Jordan and I had seen each other naked more than fifty times. This was nothing new. Plus, she didn't have A/C in her room so I welcomed the burden of clothing being lifted. I stood and made my way over to the easel, where she was still working. She didn't need my form anymore. There was too much going on in her head to even see it any longer.

"Just the obligatory self-portraits and shit they make us churn out in every basic class," I finally answered.

I took her mug from the stool next to her and sipped her wine; the bitter warm liquid burned slightly as it slipped down my throat. I watched as my features formed on the white canvas in stark, black ink. She always made me look beautiful. A woman with purpose. Like there was something behind my eyes that you wanted to know.

"Well you wouldn't have to repeat it all for the third time if you just stayed out of trouble and showed up for class," she joked as she took the thicker brush from her hair again, adding the beginnings of feathers to my hair.

"Yeah, yeah," I said, taking another swig of her drink.

"College blows," she said like she was talking about the weather.

"This is good," I said, gesturing to the work in front of us. I crossed one arm over my chest. I wasn't self-conscious before I saw the painting. But the way she depicted my body in a way that made me look beautiful, like I was some sort of inky angel, it made me that much more aware of my flaws. It made me make up new ones.

Unfazed, Jordan took the mug from me and gulped some down. "It sucks."

She always said that. "You just started. Give it a few hours, and you'll fall in love."

Her eyes scanned over the canvas and she tilted her head from side to side slowly, searching for more flaws embedded in the black and white. "Maybe," she stated.

I put my pants back on, convinced she was done having me model by the look on her face. She was stuck on this one. Anything she tried to make from here on out would only be a pale comparison to this, the new addition of Corbin-but-not-really-Corbin painting.

I slipped my bra and tank back on, tying my hair into a ponytail. Taking out my own sketchpad, I sat back down on the couch where I was before.

"So," I said.

"So..." She picked up a brush again but had yet to touch it to painting.

"Where do you get your ideas from?" I asked, scribbling with a pen on a clean white sheet of paper. Ink was my favorite medium. It was darker than any pencil could get, and there was something so final about it. You couldn't smudge a mistake away or simply erase it. The only thing you could possibly do with ink was layer more on top, try to cover it up. Even if you couldn't see the mistake anymore, it would always be there. Only you would know about it.

"What kind of a question is that?" she asked.

"Well, you know," I said, turning the light scribbles into an eye, dragging down a line into the bridge of a nose. The beginnings of lips began to emerge. "Like, do you wake up with an idea and just have to draw it so you don't forget about it, or do you just sit down at the easel and see the painting?"

Jordan shrugged, washing her brush clean in a plastic cup on her stool, wiping it off on a paper towel. "I guess a little of both."

The lips parted on their own, the mouth slightly open as if trying to form words. "You ever make something you don't remember making?"

She paused to stare at her work again. "Like, you mean get drunk and paint? Yeah, haven't you?"

I shook my head. "No. I mean have you drawn something without realizing you were drawing it and then you look down and POP, there it is?"

Jordan laughed. "I *wish*," she said. "Would save me a Hell of a lot of time. That's for sure."

I didn't have a response to that.

"Fuck it," she said suddenly, standing and placing her paint palette and brushes down. "I need a break." Sighing, she plopped down on the couch next to me. "Ooooh," she said, taking the pad from me before I even noticed she had laid a finger on the book. "Very nice."

I wasn't even looking that closely at what I was doing. I just wanted something to keep my hands busy.

"Thanks." I hated it when people looked at my work when it was unfinished.

"I'd hit it."

Swiping the sketchbook back from her, I studied my own work. I had drawn a man's face. He had an angular jaw, high cheekbones, and the beginnings of eyes that were looking through something as if they could burn through the paper. His lips were full, slightly parted, a slight smirk pulling at the corners like he had a secret.

"This what you're talking about?" she asked.

I flipped a page and started something new, too afraid to stare at the drawing any longer.

CHAPTER
THREE

THE FIRST FEW WEEKS OF summer break slipped by blissfully unnoticed. I slept in, ate junk, painted what I wanted, and basked in the glory of not having to be somewhere at a certain time. Sure, I picked up some extra shifts at my part time job at the craft store, but that was nothing. I was free from color theory, shade gradients, figure models that were anything but models, and endless stress.

At least that's what I thought. That's what I was prepared for.

They tell you to always prepare in advance for a disaster. You see those clouds looming overhead and you're supposed to board up the windows, stock up on toilet paper, and make sure you have enough candles. I was good at that. I could always see the darkness forming beneath the surface, even if all anyone else saw was a clear, blue sky.

But this had me completely off guard. I hadn't even had the chance to check if I had enough matches for those candles.

I came home from Jordan's house one afternoon, after a day full of paint and posing. I was feeling light in my summer clothes and I was happy to let the heat play on the exposed skin of my arms and legs.

When I opened the door, it was like the music suddenly stopped. Someone had ripped the needle from my record. Someone had smashed the record *in half.*

It was dark in the living room when I closed the door behind me. The curtains were drawn, the windows tightly shut and making the room stuffy yet somehow cold. My legs were suddenly heavy, not wanting to move forward.

First I heard the television. How it wasn't on a channel, but rather one that didn't come in, the black and white scramble filling the silence of the room and creating a backdrop to my mother, sitting alone on the couch, staring off into the distance. Not at the TV, but through it, like she could swim in the eerie snow and get lost, never to be found again.

"Mom?" I asked, letting my bag slip from my shoulder and *thunk* to the floor. I didn't even think about the pages of my sketchbook folding under the weight.

I watched as the TV buzzed on in front of her, the signal from the DVD player telling her it wasn't on the right channel. I turned it off, the white noise grating on my nerves. Mom continued to stare at the blank screen like I hadn't done anything, like I wasn't even there. She was still in her pajamas; the threadbare white ones with the faded blue roses on it. In her lap was the box she got me the last day of class. I hadn't even thought about the thing since she put it in my room. There was a slight scraping sound filling the room now as she slowly opened and closed the drawer; it was more unnerving than the TV had been.

"Mom?" I repeated, louder this time. It was never good when she was unresponsive. Usually it meant that she had forgotten to taken her meds or that the meds she had taken weren't working. Her blue eyes were glazed over into a dull grey as she sat on the couch amongst unfolded clothes and a few stray magazines. Her hair was still in foam curlers and it looked like she had started doing her makeup—one cheek unbearably pink and youthful with blush while the other was pale. She seemed so small sitting there, with the even smaller box resting on the thighs of her torn nightgown, like the sofa was about to swallow her whole at any moment.

I moved in front of her this time, afraid to get too close, like she was contagious. Like I could catch her insanity like mangled butterflies in a net.

"Mom?" This time when I said the word, it came out tight and strangled. But I didn't cry. I couldn't.

Last time this happened, I cried, and it didn't help anything. That was when I was around ten, and I didn't know what to do when she sat on the porch, staring at the empty lot across the street like there were people on the other side, staring at her. Now was different. I knew what to do.

Without glancing at her again, I stumbled to the kitchen and slung open the drawer, pens and stray rubber bands flying out as it nearly lifted off the track.   I flipped through the black address book she kept for such emergencies but never actually bothered to fill. It was mostly blank pages and thick stacks of business cards and Post-it notes sandwiched between the pages. I took off the thick twine she used to hold it together and frantically searched for the number of her psychiatrist. I knew by now that Mom tried to hide the number, but it was always somewhere she knew I could find, if the situation was dire enough. It was stuck between a Chinese menu and a card for a mechanic and I dialed the number instantly, barely aware of my shaking fingers or how light my head felt as I heard the static of the TV turn on again.

I jerked my head to the side, around the corner of the kitchen as the receiver rang in my ear. Mom was still in the same position she was when I left her, only now she had the remote tucked under one of her hands. So maybe she wasn't completely out of it, if she could tell that I had turned the TV off and wanted it back on. Her other hand was still in her lap, sliding the drawer of the box in and out, in and out. That sound was louder than the static from the television. Louder than the ringing in my ear. Louder still than the receptionist picking up on the other line.

"Doctor Fletcher," said the receptionist in a monotone voice.

"H—Hi," I said. "I'm calling for my mother. She's a patient of Doctor Fletcher's."

There was a pause, the clicking of some keys on a keyboard. "Name."

"Corbin," I said stupidly. "I mean Susan—Susan is my mom. Susan Greene."

"Are you making an appointment?"

"No," I said breathlessly, wishing it was that easy. "My mom, she's uh, I don't know," I stammered as I searched for the words. "She's not really responding to what I say."

"She's unresponsive?" she asked in the same monotone voice. "How long has the patient been unconscious?"

I sighed in frustration. It would have probably been simpler to call 911, but it would have cost us considerably much more money, what with the ambulance ride and all. "No," I said firmly. "Look, she's sitting on the couch staring at the TV and basically drooling on herself. What do I do?"

More clicking of keys. More silence on her end as the drawer slid in and out, in and out. The TV hummed with snow, Mom's eyes became farther and farther away from the room she was sitting in.

"Alright, I'll ask the doctor."

I opened my mouth to respond, but I was put on hold; some light rock music station playing smooth pop piped through the phone. I glanced at Mom again. No change.

I felt more alone now that there was no one to talk to, now that my mom was no longer my mom.

The music cut off and the line clicked before a male voice answered. "Miss Greene?"

"Yes!" I said, startled by the sudden humanity.

"Here's what we're going to do," he said calmly. I imagined him in a polo shirt underneath his white coat, large coke bottle glasses and a receding hairline as he sat at the receptionist's chair, shooing her off with a silent hand as she was banished to the file room or something. "I'm sending an ambulance to your house and they're going to take her to Cedar Ridge. It'll be covered by her insurance, okay?"

He spoke like we were on the same level, and I wanted to believe we were. We were sane, healthy human beings. We were working together to be of help to someone unlike us, someone who so desperately needed the help of people such as us.

"Okay," I said.

"I'll meet her there for an evaluation," he said. "And I'll update you once we have a clear idea of what's going on."

I sniffed, barely aware of the unshed tears stuck in my throat. "Is she... is she going to be okay?"

"Oh yes," he said. Now I imagined him signing off on all of his official forms for the day, one hand wrapped around a heavy pen, one shrugging on a coat despite the heat outside as he wedged the phone between his shoulder and ear. "It's most likely a side effect," he said. "We'll adjust her meds and then see how she is."

He said it all so simply, like he was baking a cake and the first time around there were egg shells in the batter so he decided to have another go at it.

"O...kay," I said, forcing myself to take a deep breath. "So what do I do?"

"Just wait for the ambulance and leave your mother where she is, so long as she's not hurting herself. Pack her an overnight bag with all of her current medication and a change of clothes.

No belts or shoelaces, alright?"

His words spun around me like flies. I couldn't trap one and make it understand why I was trying to swat it away. "Okay."

"Alright. I'm going to hang up now," he said. "The ambulance should be there in a few minutes. It's going to be okay."

I didn't say anything until I heard the click of the phone going dead on the other side. I couldn't move until the dial tone buzzed, shaking me out of my stupor. I slammed the phone down and sped into Mom's room, tripping over boxes and various other objects I never bothered to take too close of a look at since they had become permanent fixtures. I pulled the suitcase from under the bed after clearing the space of other debris. Then I set to work with the clothes.

Something hard crunched under my foot and I guessed it was a CD case or something else made out of heavy plastic. I couldn't be concerned with it at the moment. I slid open drawers and only thought of Mom on the couch, sliding the box open and closed, open and closed. I shoved some clean underwear, a few T-shirts, and a few pairs of pajama bottoms for her along with her favorite yellow robe. I took out the drawstrings and left the sash to the robe on the floor. I didn't want to think about why the hospital didn't allow her to have strings like this. I already knew.

After packing a pair of slippers and the current book she was reading on her nightstand, I lugged the suitcase out of the room and set it by Mom's feet. She was staring at the TV, the box now sitting quietly between her hands.

"Mom," I said, kneeling down in front of her and blocking

her view. "Mom, you're going to the hospital." If anything could have made her jump off from the couch, it would be that. "I called Doctor Fletcher and he called them, okay?"

She stared through me, like the snowy screen behind me could be seen directly through my chest. "It won't cost any money, so that's good, right?" I tried to employ the same, matter-of-fact tone the doctor had given me, but it didn't seem to be holding out too well.

It was quiet for a long time then, as Mom's glassy eyes stared straight ahead and the TV flickered in the dim room. Once again I was struck with the thought of how small she looked. How she didn't seem like my mom or even a person at all, just a shell. A car with no one behind the driver's seat.

I took the foam rollers gently out of her hair, one by one, releasing tight curls that were still damp in the center. "There," I said when I was done, fluffing the curls around her face. They were silky and soft under my fingers. "That's better."

But not quite. I stood and tossed the foam pink curlers onto the coffee table, on top of the dusty candy dish that held loose change. I flicked on the light and turned off the TV once more, this time setting the remote on top of the mantle, where I knew she couldn't reach it without standing and walking over to retrieve it. Then one by one I pried her cold fingers from the warm wood of the box in her lap.

I was still holding it when I saw the red and white revolving lights outside the window, when two paramedics dressed in blue carried her out by hand, one holding her feet, one lifting her under the arms—there wasn't enough of a path for them to slide the stretcher in. They assured me that her vitals were good, that she would be at the hospital for a few hours of observation before they transferred her to Cedar Ridge, where the situation would be in their hands. Then they asked me if I'd like to ride in the ambulance with them.

Unconsciously, I clutched the box to my chest, the hard wax around the latch pressing into my sternum. "No," I said with a shaky voice. "I'll wait for the doctor to call me."

They didn't pass any judgment, but I wanted them to. I wanted them to tell me what a horrible child I was for not wanting to see this through, to wait in the hospital and fluff her pillows until she was once again my mother. But they didn't. They set my mom on the gurney just outside of the house, strapped her in, and wheeled her into the back of the truck, closing the doors and driving off.

CHAPTER
FOUR

THE FLIES CAME NOT LONG after Mom left. They appeared in the night, like the first cold wind of fall after a long summer. One morning there was sun and heat, the next, there was an endless sea of black. They stuck to windowpanes in sheets, coming down like snow with spindly legs and twitching wings. Mom may have had a lot of junk, but we never left food lying around the house. We'd never had a problem with bugs before. I thought about staying with Jordan for a few days, but that didn't seem right. Mom had barely been gone two days and I was already jumping ship. Last time she went away, I ran off to Philly by myself and just wandered around for the two weeks she was locked in some ward. I took all of my savings and stayed in hotels with clean white sheets, sparse decorations, and mints on the pillows. I saw shows and went to galleries. I didn't think about what was going on at home.

It was incredibly selfish. If Mom was suffering, shouldn't I?

What made me so special?

The thing about the flies was that they weren't *inside* the house. They merely clung to the screens of the windows, blocking out the sun. The low buzzing of their collective wings rubbing against each other was the only real nuisance.

There was no need to leave. It was just some freakish mating thing and it would go away soon enough.

Still, when I lay awake at night, it wasn't something I could exactly ignore. It wasn't that they were particularly loud, or that I was even all that grossed out by them. It was that when I listened to them, clinging to the thin barrier between outside and my bedroom, I was almost...comforted.

I was alone in the house. Surrounded by so many things: glass, porcelain, stuffed things with eyes that stared back with dead gazes. Knowing that there was something alive on the other side of the curtain made it bearable.

Corbin, came the voice.

I hadn't realized I had been without the voice until it whispered by my ear. As if someone was lying next to me, murmuring as they laid their head on the pillow to my right.

I took a deep breath and released it when I didn't hear anything else.

Not wanting to turn around and find no one there, I brought the blankets closer to my body. I turned even more onto my left side, staring at the unlit nightlight on the wall. The bulb had gone out a few days ago and since Mom wasn't home, no one bothered to change it.

Somehow, I wasn't comforted by knowing the voice had gone. I felt lonelier than ever.

Darkness. Most people are afraid of it. I always kind of liked it. I was the one who, when all of the neighborhood kids got together to play hide and seek, chose the closet. The crawlspace. The shed behind the house. When other kids my age were asking their parents to check for monsters under the bed, I was begging my mom to not leave the door open a crack after I fell asleep while she read me my bedtime story. If there were monsters under my bed, I sure as hell wanted to see them.

Nightmares also never really scared me. I never woke up in the middle of the night and snuck into my mother's bed. I wasn't afraid of going back to sleep for fear of falling back into the same dream, picking up where I left off before I woke up.

Bad dreams were fuel for my mind. If something scared me, I used it. I painted it, drew it, sculpted it from clay or wire. You can manipulate anything if you choose to. I could either drown in fear when the black cloud of sleep weighed me down, or I could welcome it. Invite it into me and take note of every detail so I could save it for later.

This dream—if it was a dream—was different.

Corbin. The voice came again in the dark. I couldn't tell how much time had passed between the first time it said my name and now, but I was asleep. I knew that much. My entire world was cast in black, like I had closed my eyes and not yet opened them when I retreated into my mind. The voice was somehow different here. Deeper, fuller, more real.

"Who are you?" I asked. "Why do you keep saying my name?" My voice was flimsy.

I wanted to feel around, but I didn't have hands. I didn't have a body. I was just my mind in the dark. That was it.

There was a low humming. It sounded like different languages switching back and forth. French then Russian, then a low whisper that I couldn't make it out at all.

"Hello?" I said. "Are you going to answer me or what?"

Somehow, in dreamland, this seemed only logical.

Corbin, it said, not quite as full as the first time. More of a gentle whisper. *Little crow. Dark haired beauty.*

The bed shifted next to me, but I couldn't be bothered to open my eyes. "You're not real," I said into the darkness.

Something brushed past my face, just below my lip. It was neither warm nor cold, just a presence of slight pressure and then nothing.

But I am *real, Corbin*, the voice said in a whisper. *In time, I will show you how real I am.*

I took a deep breath. This was crazy. But I was also all alone, so even though I was scared of what hearing this voice meant, I was comforted that it was here with me.

"What do you want?" I asked.

Murmuring. Light voice on top of light voice, speaking over one another in different languages and whispers of words I understood, just not in this context. When it went on too long, I sighed. "Can you at least tell me who you are?"

I managed to open my eyes, staring at the blank ceiling,

shadows of the ever-present flies playing off of it. I wondered for a second if my eyes were really open or if they had only opened into a different dream. I blinked once, twice. The voices disappeared. I couldn't be sure in my half-awake state, but I felt the covers shift beside me. I didn't care that this was just my mind trying to cope with my mother leaving.

You aren't afraid of me, are you? But it wasn't quite a question.

I rolled over, exposing my back to the unseen entity. "No," I said. "I guess not."

My hair lifted off of my back gently, as if someone was running their hands through it lovingly, the way Mom used to when I was sick when I was little.

"I'm afraid of what you *mean*," I said. "I'm much too old to be playing with imaginary friends."

I felt breath on the back of my neck. It was warm and smelled of dried leaves. I melted into the scent of it, relaxing my head against the pillow. *You don't think I'm imaginary*, the voice said, so close to my ear that they sounded like they were right there, speaking directly to me and no one else. *Not really.*

I sighed. "Still," I said. "If I turn around right now, would I see you?"

There was no answer.

"Why can't I see you if you're real?" I whispered.

Again, I was met with silence.

I tried to turn around but found I was weighted. I didn't want to fight against it, but I felt that if I did, I could push past whatever force was holding me in position. *Please*, came the voice. *Don't turn around.*

"Why not?"

That slight pressure again, this time on my hand over the covers. It was like a small wave lapping over my skin before it was gone.

"Are you trying to touch me right now?"

I swallowed, unaware of when the fear had subsided and the curiosity began.

I was drifting again, falling into the scent of leaves like I was outside in autumn. Like there were trees burning all around me.

When the voice came again, it was barely there. *My name is Six.*

The last word was garbled, washing over me.

That's all I will say for now.

I couldn't take it anymore. I changed positions and opened my eyes to look at the space next to me. I knew I was awake now. When I turned on the light, there was no one there. Just a faint outline of a body in black feathers.

I combed my hands over the pink silk, gathering them up into a pile. Maybe I was dreaming after all. When I rested my head on top of them, the feathers smelled like a forest fire.

That was it. Darkness and silence for the longest time. In the waking hours, I would have been more curious, anxious to find out what was happening. But here it didn't matter. My mind was merely resting and making up voices again. This was subconscious flotsam left over from the day; nothing more.

Thank you, it whispered after a long while.

Then I was awake.

There was no slow awareness. No fluttering of the eyelids or registering of light before the realization that yet another night had passed and I had slept through the entire thing. I was simply in a deep sleep one moment and wide awake the next, staring at the sunlight as it played on the pink canopy above my head.

I blinked a few times before I moved. When I rolled over, the feathers were gone, but the box was sitting next to me, curled under my arm as if I had held it through the night.

CHAPTER
FIVE

THE SECOND WEEK WITHOUT MOM went by just as slowly as the first, only I kept my distance from the house. The flies were buzzing too loudly in the silence, the vibrations of their wings bouncing off of each and every object in each and every room. I wanted to call an exterminator, but it wasn't like we could go spending money on that sort of thing, especially if they weren't exactly *in* the house. Plus, Mom didn't like disturbances. If someone had to spray for insects, they would most likely have to shift some things around. And I didn't want her coming home just to be sent back to the hospital.

Instead, I hung with Jordan most days. I would go to work at the craft supply store and go to her house straight from work, pieces of glitter or random styrofoam fragments stuck to my black uniform pants. We painted mostly. She knew what had happened because I told her in passing, the way someone tells you where they bought their shoes six years ago. Jordan knew my mother wasn't the most stable of people from the moment she met her at one of our early art shows. It was more than a year ago, but we both remembered it and refused to bring it up ever again. Jordan had painted a surreal, humanoid spider creature sitting on a log next to what looked like a heap of white hair until you got closer. There were actually eyes staring out at you when you looked between the strands. Mom was fine until she saw that. Her psychiatrist would later tell us that it was the idea that something could be hidden in plain sight that had triggered her. He couldn't explain why Mom's reaction was to rip off our professor's glasses and smash them into the painting until both they and the canvas were completely destroyed.

I was ready to switch colleges after that. That kind of stuff happened to me throughout my school career—from elementary on. I would be damned if I would let it follow me to higher education. Fortunately, Jordan was a true friend and genuinely cared that she had me to suffer through classes with. She told the professor and anyone else who asked that it was part of a performance piece she was working on for another class. She bullshitted it so well that by the beginning of the next semester, no one even mentioned my mom, just the crazy performance artist girl.

Jordan appreciated my mom's mental state the way writers appreciated Shakespeare or the way horror movie fans appreciated Michael Myers. She fed off of my mother's mental illness and soaked up what she did so she could reproduce it in her own art. Last semester, she sculpted a vase complete with glazed flowers that almost looked real, the broken pieces of our old professor's glasses stuck between the petals.

"We should do something fun tonight," Jordan suggested, her posture changing only slightly but enough to mess up the sketch I had just started of her. I tore my newsprint from the easel, crumpled the paper, and threw it over my shoulder as I glared in her direction.

"Sorry," she said with no apology in her voice.

I knew she wasn't going to stop talking just yet, so I stopped my timer on my phone and waited.

"I'm just saying you should do something to get your mind off of all this shit," she said, emphasizing with her hands. She talked with them a lot. Jordan was the only person I knew who could act completely natural naked—the same way she would if she was fully clothed.

I pretended to pick some pencil shavings off of my pants. "And would this something also have something to do with the fact that I now have a house free for people to party in?"

Jordan shrugged but I saw right through it; not that she was trying to hide her motives in the least.

"You've been to my house," I said. "There's no room for anyone in there."

"But you *do* have a really nice backyard," she said. "And your neighbors don't live too close, and it's nice and warm out."

I sighed. It's not like I hadn't had parties at my house before when Mom was away. It was just that this time, it seemed somehow different. More selfish.

Besides dropping off some of her clothes, I hadn't been to visit Mom since she was admitted. True, we had called each other and she had repeatedly told me not to come, but I had always visited in the past. I didn't know what was holding me back this time. I just didn't want to be reminded that I was not your average college student on summer break.

"Eh?" Jordan said, her voice tugging on me and her waggling eyebrows making me smile. "What do you say?"

I stared at the blank paper in front of me, indents from the last pose imprinted on it because I had pressed too hard. "Not too many people?" I asked.

"Whatever you want," she said. "I just don't like seeing you like this." Her expression turned serious as she studied me from where she sat on the stool.

"Like what?" It wasn't like I was acting any different, was it?

"Like your Mom is in the hospital and you're trying to avoid thinking about it." She didn't look at me, but smiled. "So let's stop thinking about it, huh? Have some fun tonight. Crack a few beers, hang out with some friends, and maybe even get you to smile for more than a few seconds."

I flipped through the newsprint pad until I couldn't see the indents of my failed attempt at drawing my friend. "Okay, maybe a smile," I said. "But no laughing."

She held her hands up in defense. "Hey, no one said we were getting crazy."

I was already relaxed at the idea of having a normal night any twenty-two year old would have when their parents were out of town. "So are you done talking or what? Because I'm starting my ten minutes over again."

Jordan held a finger to her lips and resumed her simple pose of more or less being slumped over on her stool, one knee raised so she could lean her elbow against it and rest her head in her hand.

I turned one more page and found the clean off-white surface comforting as I drew with a steady hand for the first time all day.

I WENT HOME AROUND FIVE o'clock, telling Jordan I wanted to at least make sure there were enough chairs outside so people wouldn't be tempted to sit down in the house on top of anything Mom deemed important. Thankfully, there weren't many windows that faced the backyard so the flies and the buzzing were at a minimum there. Once I was done unfolding metal chairs and lugging coolers out back, I went up to my room to shower a day's worth of sweat off of me and get ready for a party. I went all out, figuring there was no point in half-assing. I shaved, lotioned, and primped until I was almost unrecognizable. I chose to wear a short summer dress and my knee-high docs. It was the nicest thing I owned and I thought it'd be stupid to wear anything else on my feet in the overgrown grass out back.

I was sitting on the floor in front of the full length mirror in my room, just about done lining my mouth in a dark plum color when something caught my eye across the room. The dark wood of the box glinted in the fading light that a gap in the blanket of flies allowed. I didn't want to think about my dream or how I had woken up with it in my arms, but I couldn't help it. Mom had just given it to me before she went away and I let it sit there, still dusty, still a grody piece of trash someone had to sell to some unsuspecting yard sale-goer.

Standing, I walked over to the box and tentatively picked it up in my hands, the wood surprisingly warm in the air conditioned room.

My feet shuffled toward my desk and I sat down, setting the box in front of me. If it was possible to feel bad for an inanimate object, it was this. The metal was tarnished, the thick red wax gluing the lid closed. I picked it up again and gently shook, hearing the same dull rattling coming from inside. It wasn't like I wasn't curious as to what was inside, it's just that I hadn't really had the time to pry open the lid; it wasn't at the top of my list of priorities.

After looking up what supplies I needed, I headed to the bathroom to grab some toothpaste and an old toothbrush—most forums discussing silver tarnish said it worked well. Next, I went into the kitchen and grabbed a butter knife, figuring I could use it to scrape off the wax.

Turning on some soothing music, I positioned the box on top of some newspaper and set to work with shining up the metal. I squeezed toothpaste onto the old brush and in tiny circles, brushed like I was trying to clean a child's freshly cut teeth. It didn't take long before the rust began to melt away, showing the shiny surface underneath. "I knew you could be pretty," I said to myself over the music, flies, and soft scraping of the toothbrush. "And now you'll be minty fresh, too."

I laughed. I tried to keep talking to myself to a minimum—that was what crazy people did—but sometimes I couldn't help it. It wasn't like there was anyone home that could walk in on me and see anyway.

Next I worked on the seal. It took longer than expected, and it smelled like an old person's house, musty and like it hadn't been cleaned in a while. Once the wax was removed from around the metal clasp holding the lid in place, I expected it to be easy to open, but found that it would not budge.

The clasp opened without incident, but the actual lid was going to take more work. I tried wedging the knife between the two pieces of wood, slipping a few times and smashing my fist into the desk. I got the knife between the wood and gently pried, making my way around the edges carefully, not wanting to crack the wood or bend the metalwork.

With a loud suction sound and a pop, the lid finally fell open, finally revealing what it was inside:

Nothing.

PEOPLE STARTED ARRIVING at nine. Jordan had taken it upon herself to bring an MP3 player and speakers, positioning them by the door so we could hear whatever she wanted. Currently, she was playing Animal Collective and it was like nails running down each and every nerve in my body. Thankfully, someone had a bonfire going and had handed me my third beer, so I was warm and kind of not caring about much.

Jordan came over to me and wrapped an arm around my shoulder. "There's someone I want you to meet," she said.

I rolled my eyes. Of course there was.

I watched as she strutted over to the tomato patch at the edge of the fence and dragged someone back toward the fire. I couldn't see them clearly until they were right in front of me.

A thin yet muscular guy with dingy green hair smiled at me through a thick beard. He was wearing tight jeans and a shirt that looked like it had been repurposed from the thrift store, and not in a good way. I wasn't sure if he was attractive, but more alcohol would leave no doubt in my mind.

"This is Chess," Jordan said for him as he stuck out his hand. "He brought the weed."

I hadn't had any of that yet; I was fine just sitting and drinking. "Oh," I said. "Cool." I reached out my hand just a few seconds too late, but he still shook it before he took the empty plastic lawn chair next to me.

"You go to Peterson's with Jordan?" he asked.

Mysteriously, Jordan had backed into the darkness again. I could hear her laugh. "Yeah," I said as his features swayed. I smiled, a warm heat flooding my cheeks. "You?"

He made a face that told me he was too good for college—I had seen it before so I recognized it—and said, "Nah. I do my own thing. What's your major?"

I shrugged as I took another sip of my beer; it was already too warm. "Right now, 2-D. No clue if it's going to stay that way."

"Cool, cool," he said, nodding like I had just told him the most interesting thing in the world. "I work mostly in spray paint."

I resisted the urge to roll my eyes. Ugh. A "graffiti artist" was rarely an actual artist in my experience. You could do so much with the medium, but most just tagged subways or walls with obnoxious bubble letters no one could read. Not wanting to prolong our riveting conversation any longer when we both knew what he really wanted, where we would end up anyway, I stood up. "You want to go inside?" I asked.

He looked surprised, but that expression quickly changed to a wide, puzzled smile. At least that was what I thought. I couldn't really see how far his lips stretched with the facial hair. "Sure."

Grabbing his hand, I ditched my warm beer and picked up a bottle of whiskey someone had brought and left unattended on the porch. "Be careful," I said as I led him through the kitchen, into the living room, down the hall, and to my room. If he cared that I lived in a den of damaged goods, he didn't say anything about it. I wouldn't be surprised if he didn't see any of it. Guys like that, once you give them the green light, they go, go, go. No distracting them from the finish line.

Closing the door and blocking out the thumping music so it was only a dull rumble, I stumbled over my boot and landed on the bed gracefully.

I took a swig of the whiskey, which was also warm but it burned enough that I didn't care.

The room was spinning. I was convinced that the house had

been set onto a carousel ride and I was just one of its unfortunate passengers.

"Don't drink much, huh?" Chess asked, sitting down next to me on the silky pink bedspread.

"Not really."

He laughed. "I've been there." He took the bottle from me, setting it down on the nightstand next to my now shiny and clean box. Noticing it, Chess picked up the box like he was some sort of art dealer. "This is..."

"Weird."

"Yeah," he said, opening the lid and closing it. "I mean, it's cool or whatever, but..."

"But it's weird."

Chess took off his faded brown leather jacket. "Yeah."

"Cool and weird."

A smirk spread across his face. "Like you."

I snorted. "Lame."

He feigned offense, even pouting for effect. "I tried really hard on that one."

Without much notice, my head was against the pillow. The world was too heavy to look at it upright at the moment. I much preferred it from this angle. "I can tell," I said. "You have shit like that written down somewhere, or do you just tuck it away for later?"

Chess lay next to me and flipped some of my hair out of my face. "You know," he said, "I can tell you're the type that likes playing hard to get."

"Who's playing?"

That smirk again.

The room spun.

The flies outside hummed so low that I doubted he even noticed.

"You're pretty," he said.

I felt my lips tug at the corners. "That's better."

Corbin.

Really. Now?

I didn't want to think. That was the whole point of this little get together, wasn't it? The whole point of bringing some guy I only slightly thought was attractive back to my room? I snatched the bottle from Chess' hands and took a swig of the whiskey, the very motion enough to make me want to vomit. But as soon as the burning in my chest cooled down, I felt fine.

"You sure that's a good—"

I broke off his sentence with a kiss. I imagined it being the most soul-crushing, passionate, all-consuming kiss I could ever muster, but it was probably sloppy and gross, too much tongue and too much force. Like I was trying to unload everything from the past few weeks into his mouth, like he could swallow anything I gave him.

He pulled away after a while to breathe and take another gulp of alcohol. When we connected again, it was like he was trying to crush everything I had just given him back down my throat.

I pulled away this time. I'd had enough of that.

Sitting up, I brushed my hair out of my face and straightened my skirt.

He grabbed onto my arm and tried to bring me back.

Corbin, the whisper said. *I can help.*

I blinked a few times.

Chess tugged again and I was on my back, staring at the pink canopy as it tilted before my eyes. The back of my skull bounced against the pillow once, twice, then settled into the fabric.

"God, you're so sexy," Chess said before he came crashing back into me, a satellite falling to earth and breaking up into a million pieces before it even made impact with the ground.

His breath was hot against my mouth, my neck. He smelled like a dead skunk and his hair felt greasy against my cheek. He drooled onto my skin like an eager dog and he panted like one, too. His full weight pressed into my lower half. I could feel his hardness against my bare thigh, and when I looked down at my legs, I could see his shoes were getting dirt on my comforter. Everything about this situation completely turned me off, yet I didn't make a move to stop it. I couldn't lift a finger in the direction of the door.

Corbin, came the voice once more.

I pushed my fingers weakly against Chess' chest as one of his legs came to rest heavily on top off my thighs. He was so heavy. I couldn't breathe under him. I didn't want this. I didn't want to do anything with this guy besides lose myself for a few meaningless seconds. This was not what I had in mind.

"Chess," I said. "Stop."

I could have whispered the words; I could have not said

them at all. They didn't reach him.

Hot, slick breath on my chest. Cold, fumbling fingers at my waist. I was sweating around my hairline. My limbs were too heavy for me to move.

"I said stop."

"Come on," he said. "You didn't bring me in here to talk."

Corbin

"Jesus Christ, shut up," I said out loud.

Chess didn't respond, but it wasn't intended for him.

I will ask one more time, said the voice.

Hands. Two hands on my breasts, pulling too hard at what lay underneath. Whiskey-damp breath in my ear, around my face as the weight of his body pressed into me. As he tried to shift my legs beneath him so he could move on to the hem of my dress.

Do you want this?

Above me, on the baby pink canopy, a stain began to form. Coffee brown around the edges, the inkblot took on a deeper black hue the closer to the middle of the fabric my eyes traveled.

My vision started to tilt along with the room around me. It didn't seem real, did it? Me and a guy I had just met in a room that had not changed since I was seven. A voice telling me it would help as my vision narrowed and tunneled around the edges, like I was speeding through a subway with nothing to protect me on all sides. Chess' fingers slipped past my stomach, grazing my hipbone.

The word escaped my lips without much effort: "No."

Then breaking. Everything was breaking. The hiss of glass

and the pound of wood against carpet. The music outside suddenly stopped, giving way to the screams of everyone else at the party. Then the buzzing began.

A slick black sheet of flies drifted into the room through the broken window. Although Chess had jumped off of me the moment he heard the commotion, I couldn't move. A fly buzzed past his ear. One flew around his ankle. He swatted them away like they didn't even matter. Like there wasn't glass all over the carpet.

Then all at once, they were on him. A blanket of black, covering nearly every inch of his skin except his face, but they were swarming fast, inch by inch, threatening to close over his mouth and suffocate him.

Chess stared back at me in horror, like I was part of this nightmare with him. I didn't move from my spot on the bed as he frantically sailed around the room, swatting and swiping his hands down his body as his panic rose, as his cockiness turned into desperate, childish screams. "What the *fuck*," I heard him say. "What the fuck, what the fuck, what the fuck!"

The sound of a thousand translucent wings drowned out everything else. I wasn't scared of the bugs. I wasn't afraid of them hurting Chess or anyone else. What I was most afraid of was the buzzing, the endless white noise and how I *liked* the sound. I backed up farther onto the bed, my back against the headboard.

What shall I do to him now? asked the voice.

I blinked a few times, scanning my eyes around the room for

the first time to look for where the voice was coming from. The box sat next to me on the nightstand, my easel stood in the corner, my plain bookshelves remained calm and white, nothing out of place. And the dirty hipster in the middle of the room flailed in front of my broken window.

"Where are you?" I whispered, the words thick on my tongue.

A freezing cold wind blew through the room, rumpling my comforter; my hair whizzed past my face. But the flies didn't move. They stuck to Chess like he was made of tar.

"Do something!" he pleaded.

Right. Suddenly standing and stumbling over the pillows that had fallen to the floor, I moved toward him. But before I could make my way around the glass, Chess was already opening the door to my room, running down the hall, and out of the house. I watched him through the broken window as he sprinted down the street, unconcerned that his car was still probably parked in the driveway.

I wanted to go to the window to see what was going on, why everyone had screamed, why the busting glass sounded as though it had not occurred just in my room.

But when I tried to take a step toward the door, I found myself taking one step back. I tried again, and I took another step backwards. Glass crunched under my boots.

Go to sleep.

I couldn't tell if this was me or the voice and I didn't really care. My eyelids were heavy. My stomach churned. If I didn't lie down, I was going to be kissing porcelain.

I crawled my barely functioning body and rapidly shutting down mind back into bed, kicking Chess' jacket to the floor like it was nothing but a piece of garbage. The comforter was cool against my skin in contrast to the heavy heat flooding in through the window. My world was still spinning, and I just wanted to close my eyes. I would think in the morning. I would rationalize it all in the morning. Things always looked different by morning; that was what I had to believe.

Rolling over, I stared at the box on my night table. I watched how the newly polished silver glistened in the dim light of my room. I reached out with my hand and felt the cold material under my fingertips and slid the drawer in and out a few times. Then I opened the lid.

A single black feather sat inside of the red velvet.

I closed the box with a snap and turned off the light.

NO DREAMS CAME that night. One moment I was in the dark, the next, the sun was blazing into the backs of my eyelids, turning my entire world a shade of red-hot pink. I rubbed the gunk from my eyes, inching gingerly up against the headboard, already dreading what I would be greeted with. When I opened my eyes, the sun was shining clearly through the windowpane, the shades opened slightly. There were no flies clinging to the surface, no broken glass on the floor.

My head pounded against my skull and I cursed myself for not drinking any water the night before. But the pain was a small character in the cast of my quickly unraveling mind.

Where was the glass? Where were the flies?

Stepping out of bed, I barely glanced at the box, not wanting to convince myself to open it. The carpet was cool against my bare feet. Though I didn't remember changing out of my clothes last night, when I looked down at myself I was only in my underwear and bra. I must have gotten overheated and stripped off the layers in my sleep.

Slowly, I inched toward the door, cracking it open barely an inch before stepping into the hall, through the house, and into the backyard.

Besides a few empty plastic cups and beer cans outside, there was no evidence that anyone had even been there the night before, let alone screaming as the windows caved in and the flies infiltrated the house like nocuous fumes.

I stepped back inside and my hand grazed the window above the couch, my fingers coming away with a fine film of dust.

"What the hell…?" I whispered under my breath.

My head pounded, the imminent hangover making itself known. I grabbed a glass of water from the kitchen and shuffled my way back into my room, sipping the water before setting it down and covering myself back up under the comforter. I didn't realize the box was in my hands until I was opening the lid, staring at the slick, black feather against the red inside.

CHAPTER
SIX

I BROUGHT MOM HOME ON Sunday—on time and exactly two weeks after she had checked into the hospital. I waited outside the stone building and watched people leave in wheelchairs and on crutches before I saw her, wearing the same robe she had on when she left. The only difference now was the blue hospital scrubs underneath. She looked like she had been away at war, not a mental health facility. What I hated more than Mom going away was Mom coming home. We didn't even really talk the whole ride; she was so doped up she couldn't really do much besides stare.

The flies had left the night of the party. Besides having to clean up a few cans and bottles, there was no evidence that it even happened. I wanted to tell Jordan about it, but telling her would be somehow admitting that I *believed* it.

I settled Mom in the living room on the only clear couch in front of the TV, which I turned on low so there was more than just our silence. "Are you okay?" I asked.

Her eyes shifted up to me from the screen. "Oh, fine, sweetheart," she said, adjusting one of the throw pillows behind her head. "I was just a little nervous this morning, so they gave me a little something before I left."

I tucked an afghan around her shoulders and handed her the remote. "You hungry?" I asked.

She shook her head. "Just come sit with me a while."

Mom shifted her legs to the side so I could sit next to her. She reached out and brushed the back of her hand against my cheek. "You look so tired, Corbin," she said. "Do you feel alright?"

Shrugging away from her touch, I took her hand in mine and set it between us. "I'm fine," I said. "Just some trouble sleeping is all."

Mom closed her eyes a moment, as if the room was spinning around her and she needed to steady herself. "You should see someone about that," she said, turning her attention to the TV, where some rich housewives threw wine in each others' faces on screen before it cut to commercial.

"I'm fine," I repeated.

"That's how it started with me," she mumbled, drifting somewhere between sleep and wakefulness.

I sat up straighter. "Really?" I asked, not wanting an answer.

Her head lolled to one side. "Sure," she slurred. "Insomnia, then irritability, then hallucinations...but you know all that."

You are not the same, Corbin, the voice said from behind me. I knew there would be nothing there when I turned around so I didn't bother. That was exactly what a crazy person's mind would want to think.

Mom's eyes opened into slits. "Sweetie, I think I'm going to rest a while."

I waited until she was breathing evenly with her eyes closed before I disappeared into the kitchen to see if we had anything to make her to eat when she woke up.

I stared out the window above the kitchen sink. Mom had hung three different sets of wind chimes from the ceiling there; one made of shells, one made of wood, and one made of the traditional metal. When a slight breeze swept through the room, it sounded like the earth was trying to deliver a personal chaotic message that no one could understand.

I opened the fridge and found nothing particularly edible so I closed it and stared at the many magnets on top of old macaroni pictures and paintings I had made from the time I was in preschool until now. Sometimes I would throw out sketches and find them stacked on the fridge, wrinkles and all, like Mom was just as proud of my failures as she was of my finished work.

After finding a can of tomato soup in a cabinet, I took my sketchbook and sat on the porch swing outside. The sun wasn't too harsh with a few storm clouds rolling in, and now that there was no background buzzing from the flies, I could fully concentrate on my work.

I really tried not to flip to the drawing of the mysterious man, but my fingers thrummed with excitement as if they had a mind of their own. My heart pounded in my chest, my stomach did little flips like I was jumping on a trampoline as the thick pages flew through my hands, searching for the exact place they wanted. It didn't matter if I didn't want to look, and that was what scared me the most.

His face was there, the same as before. And between his page and the next lay a small, downy black feather. I picked it up and held it as I stared at the half drawn in square jaw and partially erased full lips. The eyes peeked out at me from thick lashes that I hadn't finished yet. I just knew they were meant to be thicker.

It took less than a minute to take in the details, before I regained full control of my hands and flipped the page. I turned too forcefully. Or maybe I jumped. The book flew from my lap, landing face down on the porch's chipped light blue paint.

Frustrated and confused, I sighed, stood, and picked it up, simultaneously snapping the book closed.

Which only made black feathers fly forth, getting caught on a breeze, and landing in the dead rose bush in front of the house.

I FLOPPED INTO BED THAT night ready to turn off my mind and not have to think until the next day. The voice, however, had other plans. I didn't immediately hear what it was trying to say, just muffled whispers trying to speak over one another.

They snaked around me like the fog left over from a long night of rain. When I took in a breath, I was weighted, heavy, yet I welcomed it. My hair moved around my face, invisible fingers trailing down the strands and causing my scalp to tingle all over.

My lips parted in a silent word I could not grasp.

When I opened my eyes, the soft glow of the nightlight greeted me. I could still see what was in front of me, but it was dim enough that I could convince myself that what I was seeing was merely my eyes playing tricks on themselves.

In the dark, in the space between the wall and my bed, a figure began to form. At first, there was only a long dark shape, a thick line of dark matter reaching out toward me and disappearing from my line of view as the movement against my scalp continued.

"Are you finally showing yourself?" I whispered.

I blinked against the dim light and the image was still there, growing before me. Like an ink blot, there was one spot of contact near the edge of the bed and I watched as it slowly spread outward, amorphous shapes forming into a torso, frayed edges becoming smooth and almost solid.

I slowly sat up, not wanting to believe what I was seeing as my heart pounded against my chest. The ink continued to spread and the smell of leaves returned. The arm that had been near my head moved slowly, disjointedly, to the side of the thicker shape that I assumed was the torso.

Then shoulders, a neck, and a head appeared.

Do you like this form? The words were light whispers as the question caressed my skin.

I couldn't make out any features. There was just the basic shape of a man. No face, no fingers, not even a lower half with legs. Instead, the torso area just bled down into the mattress, disappearing into the pink material.

I swallowed. "At least I can see you now," I said, fighting to keep my voice even.

More murmurings, as if the thing was conferring with itself before it spoke again. *I cannot stay this way for long.*

I blinked a few times, already noticing how the black was fading into a grey. "Why are you here?"

The nightlight dimmed and flickered behind it before returning to normal. *You need to say my name,* it said. *You remember it, don't you?*

Six. It was instant and fluid, like it was ready to rush out of my mouth. But I didn't say it. I was suddenly very tired and just wanted to go to sleep.

"Why?"

There was a long pause, the form shifting like it was underwater. More whispering, more deciphering. *I do not give many my name,* it said.

That wasn't exactly an answer, but what was I expecting? This was my mind we were talking about. If I had made this thing up, it was only natural that it would be cryptic and not tell me anything directly. I could keep up the illusion longer that way.

I rolled onto my opposite side so I was no longer staring in the shadow's direction. "I need to go to sleep," I said mostly to myself.

The mattress springs creaked. A weight lifted off of them. Then there was nothing but the black, floating abyss that had become sleep.

I HATED THE TASTE OF cinnamon. It was too spicy sweet, not knowing which flavor to side with. It reminded me of Christmas, of children pulling red sleds in the snow. Of happiness that couldn't be broken and a family that loved me.

Our tree was always one to beat. Since I could remember, Mom insisted that Daddy get a real one, one that was full and dark green. And the smell. It had to smell like pine or it wasn't good enough. All three of us sat at the kitchen table and crafted handmade ornaments out of gingerbread, cutting holes at the tops with straws so that once they were baked, we could string green and red ribbon through and hang them on our tree. Daddy loved the idea of having these ornaments next to the popcorn and cranberry strings. Mom always joked that he only wanted a tree that he could eat off of.

I was little. My shoes were black polished patent leather and I wore a red velvet dress with white lace trim. It made me feel like a princess and I insisted that Daddy buy a matching rose when we were at the supermarket earlier that day buying last minute groceries. Daddy had bought it, and he had also bought me a piece of candy as long as I promised to stay in the living room watching TV while he was in the garage, doing something secretive. I suspected it had something to do with the bike I had put on my Christmas list.

Our house was much larger then. Nothing huge. We weren't millionaires. Or maybe it was the lack of clutter and how small I was that made the space look so vast. If I tried hard enough, I could imagine getting lost in that house. Slipping into some dark corner no one ever dusted or under the rug everyone stepped over on their way from room to room, having become so much a part of the scenery that no one noticed it anymore.

I was watching *How the Grinch Stole Christmas* when the phone rang. I knew I wasn't supposed to answer, but when it stopped and started again and again, I just wanted to make the sound stop so I could continue my movie uninterrupted.

"Hello, sweetie," Mom's voice said on the other end. "Where's Daddy?"

I took the cinnamon stick candy out of my mouth so I didn't have to speak around it. The white and red stripes made it look like it was supposed to be mint flavored, but I was pleasantly surprised to find that was not the case. Wherever my mouth had touched, everything had blended into red. Mom hated when I ate junk before dinner and Daddy made me promise it would be our little secret.

"He's in the garage," I said.

There was some muffled sound on the other end of the phone, but I was unconcerned about it. In the living room, The Grinch was formulating his plan as to how to steal Christmas and I wanted to know what happened next.

"Well, can you go get him, honey?" she asked. "I'm going to be a little late and I need to ask him a question about dinner."

I knew it was important to Mom to be in charge of the meal. Holidays were a chance that she got to show how much she cared about us by feeding us until our stomachs burst.

"Okay," I said, hopping off the stool I had used to grab the phone and running over to the garage door. I turned the handle and was met with the dimly lit, oil stained, gasoline scented cement room. It had always given me the creeps, but right now it was somehow even scarier. Dad's car sat in the middle of the garage. There were no lights on. If he was in here, why was he in the dark?

I thought maybe he had heard me. That he wanted to hide so I didn't find out the present he was trying to hide. The only logical explanation was that he was somewhere in the car, but I pretended to look elsewhere first. I was under the workbench, around the corner, then finally tiptoeing around the car. I held the phone against my chest so Mom wouldn't hear when I scared the stuffing out of him. She hated it when we played pranks on each other. But this could be our little secret too. Daddy and I were good at keeping secrets.

Unable to see through the windows at my height, I wrapped my tiny hand around the handle and pulled. I had to tug really hard at the door to get it open, and when it finally gave way and opened with a squeak, I almost fell backward.

"Daddy," I said, taking the candy out of my mouth again so I could tell Mom I found him. "I got you—"

When I looked into the car through the open door, Daddy was there. I was not surprised. What I *was* surprised to find was a girl that looked like she could be my older sister sitting on his lap, nothing covering her except a green plaid skirt.

That was the day I started hating cinnamon. The day the house smelled like burned turkey and I never got to finish the movie. The Christmas Mom and I spent in a hotel where they served us stale bagels and the only present I got was from her— a small stuffed bear she had bought at the gas station the night before. When we returned home several days later, Daddy had disappeared. He hadn't left a note. He hadn't called. He didn't even say goodbye.

I sat in the living room in front of our tree, the cookies that no one ate casting shadows onto the carpet from the white twinkle lights. I watched as Mom tore every last one off of the branches and into the garbage. I watched as she cried as she took a bite of one I had made myself. Then she turned and retreated into her and Daddy's room.

I ROLLED OVER CLUMSILY, KNOCKING my phone off my nightstand and groaning. My head hurt, and it felt like I had just closed my eyes but it was morning. I stretched slowly, my muscles aching. Determined to not think of anything that happened the day before, I stood up.

No more than three seconds passed before I realized how hot it was in the room, how the window was opened and the air conditioning turned off. Mom must have been having some side effects of her new meds and feeling cold. There were bigger things to worry about other than my own mental state. After all, there was nothing wrong with me. Everyone talked to themselves and had weird dreams. Birds molted in the summer, so it should have come as no surprise that there was a feather here and there. Nothing out of the ordinary here. Shrugging off my sweats and replacing them with boxer shorts, I made my way into the kitchen.

Mom was making French toast over the stove. It smelled mostly burned, but the cinnamon came through all the same. "Hungry?" she asked.

The smile she wore was lazy and tired, like she had rehearsed it before I had even woken up. She was wearing new pajamas—flannel ones under her thickest bathrobe. "Are you okay?" I asked, my head still pounding. "You feel any better?"

Mom slid a metal spatula on a nonstick pan—something she always told me not to do. There was Teflon on nonstick pans. It was such a sinister material that we couldn't even see it—it only existed in fourth dimensions, beyond the comprehension of our three. Therefore you could never trust it. Metal against metal would only scrape it into our food.

I shook my head as I shuffled over to the fridge for some orange juice. It was about to expire, but it would have to do. I sat down at the table, not even bothering to clear a space as I drank directly from the carton. I was so thirsty.

When Mom turned around, concern was etched onto her face like I had lit myself on fire in front of her. "Corbin, you look awful!" She dropped the spatula and came over to me, feeling my head with the back of her hand. "Is everything okay?"

I snorted. I couldn't tell her yes and I couldn't tell her no.

What point was there to any of it? I took another gulp of orange juice, the pulp sticking to my teeth.

Mom inched away slightly. "Sweetie, you really don't look good," she said. Her voice was taking on that slight trill it did when she was worried about things out of her control, like her mental health or the house payments. "Maybe you should go to the doctor."

She retrieved her toast from the stove quickly, sitting across from me at the clearer spot and shoving newspapers and knick-knacks aside. She didn't touch her food.

"Corbin," she said softly after a while. "Sweetie?"

I was staring at the tabletop. The same one we'd had since I was little and didn't notice things like the color of the dining room table. It was dark oak with even darker rings fanning through it. The finish was probably once shiny, but now it was dull; scratched, and gouged in places with water stains and scars.

I finally looked up at her and she was nervously biting the inside of her cheek so I couldn't see that she wanted to bite her lip. Her eyes didn't have the normal dark circles underneath. Her cheeks were full and pink. Right now, she was the epitome of health, mental or otherwise. I didn't want to make her life complicated once again.

"I'm fine, Mom," I said, my voice hoarse, throat sore. "I'm just really tired and I feel a little nauseous."

She reached across the table and felt my neck and forehead with the back of her hand. "You should go lie back down," she said. "I can bring you soup in a little while if you want. Chicken and stars, right?"

This was what she brought me when I was small, when she wasn't feeling well, or on the rare occasion that I was sick.

Standing automatically, I left the carton on the table on top of the newspapers, near Mom and her untouched breakfast. My legs were lead, my feet sticky. I headed back to my room where I stared at all the pink and stuffed animals. I wanted to rip it to shreds. I wanted to stain everything the color of coffee that had settled in the bottom of a pot. I wanted to rip heads off of dolls and bears. But it all took too much energy. It was all too much for me to muster with my motor skills out the window.

Instead, I curled up under the blankets and laid my head on the pillow. The voice was absent for once, and I was grateful.

CHAPTER
SEVEN

I GAVE IN AND WENT to the doctor the beginning of the next week. I hadn't been sleeping at all and I felt like shit during most of my waking hours; I had muscle aches, migraines, vomiting, and a whole slew of other symptoms. I told the doctor I had some kind of summer flu, but she told me it was just a virus and there wasn't much she could do about it. So two hundred dollars and no closer to any way of feeling better later, I was lying in bed, calling out of work, and making my mother worry.

Jordan came to visit Saturday—the only night I could convince my mom that I was fine and she could do her normal all-day-weekend-yard-sale-scouting and then drinks with friends. Jordan was standing in my doorway, interrupting my endless Netflix marathon. Her hair was in two short pigtails so she could hide how dirty it was and she wore her usual painting clothes. Under her arm were all her supplies.

I opened my mouth to protest.

"I'm not taking no for an answer," she informed me, plopping her stuff down by my desk and proceeding to set up.

Shutting my laptop and sitting up in bed, I said, "I'm sick."

She snorted. "Yeah, yeah."

I didn't know if she believed me, it didn't matter. When Jordan was in a painting mood, there was no stopping her.

The Nyquil I had taken hours before was making my head spin more than usual, so when I stood to take my seat next to her I had to hold onto the desk for extra support. "Okay, but I'm not getting naked."

Jordan was leaning down, adjusting the height of her easel. "Yeah, you say that now." She wiggled her eyebrows.

I couldn't help laughing. After over a week of nothing but sleep, reruns, and the only human interaction as Mom asking if I was okay or needing anything, it was nice to have a normal conversation.

Without another word, she turned on the music—some overly-whining boy set to ukulele—and we got to work. I tied my hair in a loose ponytail, just to get it off of my damp neck. I wasn't hot or cold, just constantly in a state of sweating too much. Taking my sketchpad and opening to a blank page without looking at anything else, I grabbed my pencils and stared out the window, unable to think of anything to draw.

"So," Jordan said, the soft strokes of her brush on the canvas breaking up her speech. "Chess can't stop talking about you."

My fist froze around my eraser. We hadn't really talked about the party at all. I knew she and everyone else who had been there didn't have any recollection of the flies or breaking glass. No one said anything about it, but I was always scared that it really had happened.

Touching pencil to paper, I pretended to be preoccupied. "Oh yeah?"

"Yeah. It's kind of pathetic," she said. "You didn't give him your number?"

I shrugged. "Nah."

"Well," she punctuated the word with a long, wet brush stroke. "He won't stop texting me, asking when he can see you again."

Anger bubbled in my belly. I didn't like him talking to my friend like I was some innocent, high school crush. My stomach became hot, my hands hard to keep from shaking. "Fuck that asshole."

"You don't like him?" She actually seemed surprised. Then again, Jordan went for anything that had a pulse and smelled good. It was a plus if they understood modern art or had connections at some exhibition.

"Nope," I said, trying to keep my tone even.

She paused for a few moments. "Well that's not what I heard," she said under her breath.

There it was again, a flash of heat down my neck, my fingers shaking so much that I dropped my pencil. It didn't matter anyway; I was already kicking the chair behind me and standing so I was right in front of Jordan.

My intention was to tell her that Chess was a liar, that he had tried to take advantage of me in my drunken state and that he was a scum-bag she should steer clear of, but that all went out the window, the words too flimsy to even make it past my mouth. My vision tunneled and blurred, my hands coming into contact with something solid before I could see again.

Thick. That was the word. The air was thick. Dense, like it wasn't air at all. We were underwater. We were in space. We were somewhere that was not my bedroom and not my house. Not my street, not my life.

Jordan was on the ground next to her spilled paint water, which was soaking into the carpet in a sickly brown. She stared up at me, holding her lip. She didn't say a word and that was what scared me most. When Jordan was mad, she yelled. She yelled a lot and she used curse words you never knew existed. But when she was hurt—genuinely hurt—she said nothing. The air was so thick she couldn't get her words out of her mouth in order to reach me.

"I'm so sorry," I said.

Shakily, she stood up. "It's fine."

She was annoying me, sure, but I never dreamed of hitting her.

Jordan's lip was bleeding in the corner and I gave her a tissue from the box sitting on my desk. She eyed the thin paper between my fingers like it was some sort of a veil I was using to conceal another blow. Finally taking the tissue from me, she pressed it to her lip. "I guess I'll go," she said.

I was surprised at the words, but they didn't stop me from reaching out to her. "Wait," I said. I wanted to explain. I didn't know how, but I had to. "Don't go. I didn't mean to—"

As she stood, she held up a hand and silenced me. "It's fine," she repeated without looking at me. "You don't feel good and I come in here bothering you. I didn't mean to make you upset." Her voice was hollow, like she didn't even believe the words as she said them. She sniffed once and took the tissue away to look at before pressing it back to her lip. "I just want to go home now," she said quietly. "Okay?"

I swallowed. I had hurt my only friend and I wasn't sure why. I didn't even remember it. I just needed some time to figure this out, to explain what happened so she wasn't so mad at me anymore and so she would stop looking at me like I betrayed her.

"I'll come back sometime to get my stuff," she said. "And I'll talk to you later."

"Sure," I said in the same, empty way.

She nodded, checking the blood on the tissue again.

"I really am sorry," I said. "I don't know—"

"Corbin," she cut me off again. "It's fine. Okay?"

I took a deep breath and let it out. I couldn't get her to stay and I couldn't get her to listen to me. To *listen to* me. "Okay," I said quietly, defeated.

She opened the door slowly and stepped out into the hall. I heard her footsteps as they entered the living room, as she opened the door, and when she went down the porch steps and started her car. I heard her pull away with a slight screech through my half-open window. Outside, it was just beginning to get dark. There were crickets chirping, moths flying in the glow of porch lights, the sound of bullfrogs communicating with one another. So many things were alive and moving outside our safe little homes.

But inside my house, everything was still and silent. I could only hear the beating of my own heart, the pounding of my own pulse. I was alone. I knew Jordan wouldn't be calling me for a while—if ever again. Betrayal in any form was not something she tolerated. She couldn't. Forgiving people had only hurt her in life so she built up those walls for a reason. I could just imagine what was going on in her head right now. How I had somehow broken down or jumped over one of her walls and instead of pushing me back out into the wilderness, she let me stay and build my house, eat her food.

I was such a shitty friend.

Slumping back down into bed, I opened my laptop and turned out the light. The blue-green glow faded into the background of the room. I tucked one of my throw pillows under my arms and brought it close to my chest. I was unbearably cold. I wrapped myself in the silky pink blanket. It smelled like my mom's shampoo. She must have stayed to watch me one night as I slept. Although things had been good with her since she came home, I was always wondering about when the next storm was coming. As I brought the blanket closer to my face, her scent enveloped me and it was like she was trying to embrace me from beyond the grave and she wasn't even dead.

Was I just like my mother?

Was I crazy?

A laugh track played on the laptop screen as I set it on the nightstand and rolled over, shoving my face into the pillows. I put one over my head to block out any sound that might try to get to me during the night—real or imaginary. Just thinking about it—the box, the feathers, the stains that appeared and dissolved as if they were never there—it made closing my eyes all that much harder. Maybe I didn't want to be asleep, but staying awake wasn't an option either.

CHAPTER
EIGHT

THE DAMP THAT CAME WITH a morning after a heavy rain. Something soft under me, distracting my mind from the slight chill surrounding my body. There was the smell of dirt in my nostrils, thick and filled with the long dead and decomposing.

I sat straight up fully expecting to be in bed, but when I opened my eyes, I was outside. Far away from any houses or streets, somewhere there were no people, no cars—nothing but wilderness pressing in on all sides. I was in the same clothes from the day before, mud staining the knees. There were dead leaves matted in my hair, smudges of brown and black on my arms and caked into my hands. I sat up straighter. It looked as if I had dug myself a bed in the middle of the forest floor and went to sleep like some kind of animal making a den.

"Where are we?"

I silently scolded myself for making the question plural. I was alone—of course I was. Getting to my feet, I noticed that I had no shoes on, just white stained socks, like I had been walking all night in the muck. How could someone not remember that? How could someone walk through the night and not realize they were doing it at the time?

I felt around in my sweatpants pocket with trembling fingers and was thankful when I found my phone. I dialed the house, hoping Mom hadn't gone out.

She picked up in the middle of the second ring. "Corbin?" Her voice was laced in distress. "Corbin, sweetie. Where are you?"

I hadn't realized I was crying until I opened my mouth to speak. "I..." I took a deep breath so I could compose myself. "I'm fine," I said. "I just...I don't know where I am. I don't know how I got here."

I didn't want to admit this out loud, but I had no choice.

The silence on the other end was too much for me to take. I could imagine Mom slowly sitting down on the sofa in the living room as some show played in the background with the volume muted. The look of recognition on her face as she breathed a sigh into the receiver. I was just like her. Something was wrong with me and there was no way to fix it.

That only made my hysterics worse. My phone was beeping, telling me it was dying, and soon I would be alone with myself. "Mom," I said. "I'm scared."

I felt like a child again, sitting in front of the couch and rocking back and forth as Mom and Dad yelled and the smell of burned food filled the house. Christmas music that they had turned on to drown out their voices so I couldn't hear. I hated how weak my voice was. I hated that I was the one who suddenly needed help, and that the person I was asking wasn't fully equipped to deal with another set of emotional and psychological problems.

"It's okay." Her tone betrayed the comforting words. "Try to describe it for me. Can you see a road anywhere?"

"No," I said as my phone beeped again. I took a few steps forward, trying to figure out which direction I had come from. "There's just woods."

"I'm getting my keys," she said. "Do you think you went past the park?"

The park. That sounded logical. It was only a few blocks from my house and I would have been able to walk that distance during the night. I could have easily walked past the neatly manicured lawns and swing sets and into the woods that lay beyond. "Maybe," I said. "I'm not sure."

"Okay, baby," she said. "Try to walk around and see if you can find a road or some kind of landmark so I can find you." She spoke with the authority of someone who had done this before, of someone who had talked themselves through this countless times. On the other end of the phone, I heard the car start.

I broke into a jog towards a section of pine trees, dodging branches and roots as I made my way through the thick brush. There were birds chirping and the sun was up, but it looked as though it hadn't been for long. "Anything?" Mom asked.

"I'm trying," I said breathlessly. "I..."

Suddenly, there was the glint of something. At first, I

thought it was just a branch, something swaying on a light breeze. But when I blinked, it was gone.

I took a deep breath. My phone went silent.

"Mom?" I asked. "Mom?"

I slammed the useless device against the palm of my hand a few times as if it would do anything. "Fuck," I said under my breath as I placed it in my pocket.

You're going the wrong way, said the voice. *Turn around.*

I swallowed and wiped my eyes with the back of my hand. Ahead of me lay only more trees, more brush and nothing but green and dirt.

"What the hell am I doing out here?" I asked desperately. "Did you do this?"

There was no response.

"Answer me!" I yelled. "You fucking..." I was too weak to finish a decent insult.

A hiss sounded somewhere low and deep inside my chest. I had never made such a sound in my entire life. It was as if someone had opened up a hole in the earth and I was standing on the edge, staring down into the abyss, and the noise had come directly from there.

CHAPTER
NINE

UNYIELDING, UNRELENTING, BRIGHT WHITE LIGHT. I couldn't remember the last time I had been anywhere so illuminated. Until this very moment, I had been left in the dark, content to sit in the shadows with myself and my own thoughts and delusions. I was comfortable there, wrapped up in my little cocoon of voices and burned leaves.

When I opened my eyes, I was in a very white room. I was in a bed with white sheets pulled up to my shoulders and tucked in on all sides, making it nearly impossible for me to move much of anything besides my head. To my left was a shiny plastic nightstand with a pink cup and matching pink plastic pitcher. To my left was a window with plain white curtains set into a plain white wall. If my eyes traveled upward, I could see that there was a tall metal pole with a think clear tube trailing up to it. Attached to that was a large bag filled with some kind of clear liquid, which dripped into a reservoir, down the tube, and into me, where there was a needle somewhere under the blankets in my arm or hand.

My tongue was dry and my head felt tethered to the mattress, but I slowly shifted to a sitting position. When I looked around the rest of the room, an equally white and shiny linoleum floor surrounded the bed. The only thing breaking up the white was a dark brown door ahead of me. Rubbing my eyes with the back of my hand, I pulled the sheets from around my legs. It seemed impossible with my heavy fingers and pounding head. Maybe what was dripping though my veins wasn't just a clear liquid after all.

When I was uncovered, I could see that I was in a white gown with dark blue dots patterned around the fabric in order to look like crude flowers. I wasn't wearing anything underneath. No socks or shoes either.

I wondered where my clothes were, how I had gotten to the hospital, and who had found me. But more importantly, I wanted out. If I was here, that meant they would ask questions. Whoever *they* were. I didn't want to give anything away. I didn't want them to tell me the truth: that I was crazy. That whatever had bored little wormholes through my mother's brain wasn't circumstantial, but hereditary.

Shaking the thought from my head, I concentrated on standing. My feet were sweating against the cool floor, and my arm shook as I pushed the IV stand out of the way. Sitting on the edge of the now unmade bed, I looked down to where I was attached to the plastic bag. There was a large square of white tape in my hand, holding the needle in place. My knuckles were scratched up like I had dragged them against cement.

I didn't hear the door open.

"Miss Greene," a voice said. "You shouldn't be out of bed."

I looked up, my heart pounding loudly in my chest.

There was a large woman dressed in dark blue scrubs, her dark hair in a ponytail. She was coming toward me, her arm outstretched to wrap around my shoulder. "Now, get back into bed," she said in an almost motherly way.

I stared at her, but didn't move.

She wasn't prepared for this; she stared right back at me, waiting.

"Where am I?" I asked with a hoarse voice.

I remembered the phone call before everything faded away, my mother's voice on the other end as she tried to conceal her panic. The line going dead and falling in the woods. "My mom..." I said out loud. She must have been so worried.

"She's in the waiting area." Again, her arm came close in an attempt to usher me back to the bed. My legs were too weak to push against her and resist. My legs were back under the sheets, my head back against the pillow. She tucked me in just as tightly, if not more securely than I had been before.

"How did I get here?" I asked as she fluffed the pillow and poured me a glass of water from the bedside table. "Drink this," she said. "You've been out a while."

I took the water and gulped it down. "How did I get here?" I repeated.

"The doctor will be in shortly to talk with you," was all she said as she took the plastic cup from me, setting it back down on the side table with a hollow sound.

I blinked a few times as she turned some dial on my IV. I prayed she wasn't increasing the speed of the drug. I didn't want to be drugged. I wanted to be home.

"Now you just rest," she said in a way that told me she had in fact upped my dosage. "You'll see the doctor and then your mother when you wake up, I promise." The way she said it told me that she placated people like this on a daily basis.

"When can I leave?" I asked.

She was halfway to the door, but turned and said, "That's up to the doctor," before she vanished.

I sighed as my brain became fuzzy. The tiles on the floor bled into one another, sharp lines against cool, smooth linoleum. I tried to untuck myself again, but it was no use.

It was quiet in my room. No one talking to me and no one nearby. I wondered if they were trying to keep me all alone for some sick purpose. To watch and see if I would start talking to myself so they could point and tell me everything that was wrong.

A slight hissing came from somewhere at the back of my head and at first I thought it was the air conditioning, which was on full blast and making me cold, but it didn't stop. It only grew louder, accompanied by the smell of leaves and earth. *They cannot keep you here*, whispered the voice.

I closed my eyes tightly, wishing for once it would go away.

No one can keep you, it said directly into my ear. *No one.*

I pushed my head back into the pillow behind me, frustrated

with myself and my situation. "Why won't you leave me alone?" I whispered.

This time, when the voice came, it was right next to me. The bed dipped in near my legs. Someone was sitting right there. But that couldn't be right. Nothing inside of me could be outside.

Because you do not truly want me to go.

I swallowed, my throat drying out again. The blankets shifted around me and were brought down. *Do you want to leave?* asked the voice.

I was too afraid to open my eyes. Too scared to find myself still tightly tucked in and still all alone.

I nodded.

I can help you. The voice was back to a whisper. *I can make this go away.*

I sniffed, my sinuses feeling like they were caving in, threatening to crush my nose and make it impossible to breathe. "I want you to go away," I said, knowing that deep down, I meant that only for now. I didn't want it completely gone. I wasn't even sure why, but I didn't.

You want me to leave you when that doctor comes in, the voice said. *You want me to leave you so they do not know I am with you.*

When I opened my eyes to stare at the ceiling it spun in and out of focus. "Yes," I whispered.

The sheets came back up to my shoulders, not as tightly as they had been before. When I looked to my left, there was a black smudge in my field of vision, a dark arm reaching toward me before it faded away. When I blinked again, it was completely gone, taking the smell and hissing with it.

Closing my eyes again, I settled back into the bed, fully prepared to take the nurse's advice to rest.

Then the doctor came in.

She was a woman with brown hair cropped into a bob that framed her face. Under her white coat, she wore a purple blouse and grey pencil skirt with matching grey heels. She smiled when she saw that my eyes were open.

"Hello, Corbin," she said cheerfully, yet not so much that it was grating on my already raw nerves. "How are you feeling today?"

She produced my chart from the end of my bed and flipped a few pages, scanning them with her dark blue eyes.

"Okay," I said. "Head hurts."

She nodded to herself. "Well, all of your blood work came back normal," she said as she came over to me. "Can you sit up?"

I slowly inched upward and she helped.

She made me follow a little pen light with my eyes, turn my head back and forth, tell her the day, month, and year. The only one I got wrong was the day. I had been wandering in the woods on Saturday and it was now Monday afternoon. I had been out for nearly two days. Two days where I remembered nothing. Two days where I had no idea where I had been or what I had been doing.

She sat in a stool with wheels and flipped another page of the chart. "What's the last thing you remember before you woke up here?" she asked, pen poised in her hand as she looked at me.

"I..." I rubbed my face with the back of my hand again. "I was in the woods," I said.

"Why were you in the woods?" she asked. "Were you taking a walk?"

I shook my head, sending a sharp pain through my temples. "I woke up there...on Sunday, I think."

She scribbled something down before she looked back up at me. "And what do you remember before that?" Her tone didn't suggest that she was surprised by any of this information. It seemed like she had heard things like this every day, no big deal.

"I was at home," I said. "A friend and I painted and then I went to sleep." I knew it wasn't a good idea to omit me hitting my friend in the face with no recollection of actually doing it, but I couldn't bring myself to tell her. If I did, how the hell would I get out of here?

"Alright," she said to herself as she scribbled down something else. "So you were painting on what, Saturday?"

"Yes."

"And you woke up in the woods on Sunday? Were you with anyone?"

"Sunday morning. I was alone," I said. "I called my mom..."

"Yes," she said. "She told me you called her and she was trying to find you when the incident occurred."

I swallowed. "Incident?"

She flipped my chart back to the first page. "We aren't too sure what happened," she admitted. "The police report was kind of vague."

"Police report?"

She nodded.

"Am I in trouble?"

"Of course not," she said. "You did nothing wrong."

I sighed with relief. "So what happened?"

"You were found in the park a few miles from your house," she said. "By a child." She placed her pen in the clipboard and cleared her throat. "You were covered in mud and unconscious."

"Okay," I said. It didn't seem too bad. I had imagined I hurt someone or something.

"The police were called, and when the paramedics came, they said you were more or less face down. When they flipped you over, they found that you were covered in feathers. Black feathers."

The doctor reached into her pocket and produced a plastic baggie. She came forward and handed it to me.

I took the plastic bag from her, studying the soft material inside. "These…" I said. "These were on me?"

"There were apparently a lot of birds too," said the doctor. "Witnesses said that they were hanging off of you and the paramedics said you were unconscious. They must have thought you were dead."

I wasn't sure who she was talking about: the birds, the spectators, or the paramedics, but it didn't matter. Other people were seeing the feathers besides me and I didn't know what to do with that information. On top of that, she sounded almost amused. I hated that tone. I tossed the baggie onto the side table and crossed my arms. "So I looked almost dead but they took the time to stop and collect feathers?"

She took the plastic bag from the table and held it in her hands, studying what was inside. "It's an odd occurrence," she said. "I think they may have thought it was some kind of allergic reaction..." She shrugged. "But that doesn't seem to be the case."

I blinked a few times, refusing to say anything. Where had this doctor come from? "So I'm not in trouble," I said, "and I'm okay?"

"Yes," she said. "You may have a concussion, but your brain scans look okay and you aren't severely hurt."

I sat up straighter. "So...I can leave, then?"

She smiled slightly. "Can't wait to get out of here, eh?" She flipped my chart open once more. "I just need to ask you a few more questions."

I swallowed. "Okay."

So the questions began. I was asked to describe my sleeping habits, how I felt in general towards life, if I had trouble enjoying things like books and movies, if I ever felt like waking up was too hard. I was also asked if I ever blacked out for periods of time without any knowledge of what happened during that lost time. If there were any stressful situations in my life, if I found it hard to concentrate. If I ever had unpleasant thoughts...basically the entire psychological kaleidoscope of questions. If I turned them one way, they looked completely different, depending on whatever answer I gave the doctor.

"Alright," she said when the questions were over. "Here's

what we're going to do."

I didn't like how that sounded.

"You'll be released later this afternoon. I'm writing you a prescription for a mild sleeping pill. That should help with the stress, insomnia, and it will leave you less prone to lost time and memory loss."

I could deal with a sleeping pill. Maybe I'd sleep through the voice altogether and not have to deal with it anymore. Maybe if I just slept more, it would disappear the same as it had appeared.

"That's it?" I asked.

"That's it." She scribbled something on a light blue pad of prescription paper, ripped off the page, and handed it to me. "I want you to start taking those tonight. Allow yourself eight hours of sleep, and I want to see you two weeks from now. Okay?"

I nodded. "Can I get this taken out of my arm now?" I gestured to the IV.

"Sure. I'll have a nurse come in and get you ready for discharge. In the meantime, your mom's been asking about you. I think she brought you some clothes too."

She turned and walked out the door. I finally let out a breath. I had definitely dodged a bullet. I could have been committed to the looney bin if I wasn't careful, and here I was getting off with only a slip for sleeping pills. I could live with that. Definitely.

You don't have to take those. The voice was back almost immediately. *They will not get rid of me.*

"I know," I whispered. "But they can help me ignore you."

There was a long pause. I watched the clear liquid drip into the tube. I stared at the ceiling.

You do not want to ignore me, my love.

"What did you do?" I asked. "What happened to me?"

Again, a pause. The fading away of the voice and then the rush of a thousand whispers all trying to talk around each other. *I went walking*, it said. *I do not often go walking, but last night, I walked.*

I shook my head. "You aren't real."

But I am, Corbin, said the voice. *I am as real as you are. It will just take me longer to prove that to you than I originally planned.*

Brushing a hand through my knotted hair, I took another deep breath and let it out. The sun leaked in through the window. The birds were chirping like they had been the morning I woke up in the dirt, a bird in a nest of mud.

"Why me?" I asked. "Why do you need to be real to *me*?" I was asking myself more than anyone else, but then again, who else could I possibly be talking to?

Because you are mine, the voice whispered with certainty. *And I am yours. You are the beginning and the end of my world.*

A dry laugh worked its way up my throat and out of my mouth. "I'm not that important," I whispered.

There was no answer after that because the door opened again. Mom came into the room, rushing to the side of the bed with a pile of neatly folded clothes in her hands. "Oh, baby girl," she said as she pushed the hair from my face. "You look like hell."

I pried the jeans and T-shirt from her arms as she wrapped me in a tight hug. "I'm fine, Mom," I said into her shoulder.

"Sorry I scared you."

She sat by my legs, readjusting the sheets so they were once again covering me. "What did the doctor say?"

The way she asked the question was like she was asking if I had cancer; like she had been informed of some mass in my body, but not if it was malignant or benign.

"She thinks it's from insomnia," I said. "Memory loss and missing time. Stress and stuff," I said vaguely on purpose, not wanting to upset her.

"Insomnia?" she asked. "But you've never had trouble sleeping."

I shrugged. "I have been lately," I admitted. "And the end of the semester stuff probably didn't help any."

Mom seemed to consider this awhile before she answered. "I guess so. But are you sure you're okay?" she asked. "The doctor said it's nothing to worry about?"

I showed her my slip of blue paper, the thing that would get me back home if only the nurse would come and unhook me from everything. "I'm supposed to take these at night before bed, then come back in two weeks. But she said I'm fine."

Mom pressed a hand to her chest in a relieved gesture she must have seen in every sitcom. "I'm just happy you're okay," she said. "I was so worried."

"I know," I said as she brought me in for yet another hug. "I'm sorry."

"Promise you'll take better care of yourself," she said when she finally broke the embrace. "Okay?"

"I promise," I said, like that would solve anything.

MOM AND I BARELY SAID a word to each other on the way home. We both knew what we were thinking. That I was slipping, becoming more like her. I wanted to ask her so many questions, but if I did, I would be admitting to her as well as myself that something was seriously wrong.

CHAPTER
TEN

THAT NIGHT, I TOOK THE sleeping pill and sat on the edge of my bed, staring at the carpet as I waited for it to start working. I scratched at the tape on my left hand, the gauze underneath doing nothing but irritating my skin.

You're going to hurt yourself, said the voice. *Leave it be.*

Finally, I just ripped off the tape and threw it on the ground. At least my skin could breathe now.

You're sad, said the voice.

I rolled over, my head heavy from my spanking new meds. My room spun around me in the dim glow of the nightlight. "Yes," I whispered.

Something stroked my cheek, a phantom hand, smooth knuckles against my skin. *You are healthy,* it said. *You are not hurt.*

"But I'm crazy." I laughed to myself silently as I lay against the pillows. I figured the medicine made me loopy if I stayed awake through it. I covered myself with the sheet, hoping sleep would just suck me in.

The bed dipped. I watched as the pink silk shifted into a divot, making an indentation big enough for a human body. I blinked a few times, yet it stayed exactly as it was. I still knew I was imagining it. This wasn't real. None of it was. The only thing that was real was me and my falling apart. Piece by piece, I was crumbling.

I felt the warm tears on my cheeks, and I curled on my side, away from the spot on the bed where I knew no one sat.

The covers around my shoulders slipped down slightly. *Keep your eyes closed,* said the voice.

I laughed again as the tears fell more heavily, an endless torrent of silent sadness in the dark. I laughed at the ridiculousness of it all, the absurdity. At how much I wanted whoever or whatever it was to comfort me.

My eyes were already closed; I didn't have the energy to keep them open and stare out into the emptiness. The springs underneath me creaked quietly. The blanket was repositioned over my shoulder. There was a slight pressure around my waist and warmth at the nape of my neck. It was as if someone was hugging me, keeping me close to their chest. Then the smell of leaves came. I had come to feel safe with that smell.

"You're not real," I whispered more for myself than whatever I was talking to. "I made you up so I wouldn't be alone or something." I wiped some snot away with the corner of the blanket.

The invisible grip around my waist tightened slightly. *Hush now*, whispered the voice. *No more of that. I'm here with you.*

That only made me cry harder, yet I leaned back into the embrace. What met the back of my body wasn't exactly solid, but it wasn't as if nothing was there. It was that feeling you get when you're a kid and tipping backward in your chair, thinking you're going to fall. You know instinctively how far away the floor is from coming into contact with your skull. There was the same feeling of knowing. I was sure that there was something there and it was very, very close.

I sniffed. "Where did you come from?" I whispered. "Why now?"

The hair at the back of my neck was gathered loosely and moved to the side. Warm breath on my skin, just below my ear. *You are my beginning*, said the voice, low and directly into my ear. *You brought me forth.*

"And if I turn around right now?" I asked. "Would I see you?"

There was no answer for the longest time. *You would see something*, whispered the voice. *But I do not consider it me.*

I didn't really understand what that meant. "Why won't you let me look at you sometimes but other times I can?"

Murmurs. Voices over and under each other. *I do not like this form*, came the voice. *Other times, it is tolerable.*

"What do you mean by form?"

I am Six, said the voice, this time with more of a voice behind it. It was rough and gravely, yet somehow gentle in tone. *This is not who I am.*

I swallowed down the rest of my tears, quiet for the moment. "Who are you then?" I said quietly.

I am the earth, whispered the voice. *The fire and the flood. The sun and the rain. The mouse and the crow.*

I snorted without humor. "Great. More cryptic bullshit. Way to go, subconscious."

It will be clearer in time, said the voice. *I weaken easily right now.*

Still afraid to open them, I wiped at my eyes with the back of my hand. "If I promise to keep my eyes closed, can I turn around?" My voice sounded like a whine. I hated it. I hated how desperate I was for comfort. And to be comforted by this—*like* this.

Yessssss.

I kept my eyes tightly closed as I rolled over onto my other side. The pressure around my waist only loosened for a minute before it resumed. My head sank into the pillow, the smell of leaves even stronger in my nostrils from where I was lying now. "Why do you smell so good?" I asked.

There was a low, barely audible sound. It was like the rubbing together of twigs, the brush of legs against tall, dry grass. *You like my scent, little crow?* whispered the voice.

"Yeah." I sniffled so I could smell more.

If I am not real, how do I have a scent?

My eyes shifted back and forth under my lids, but I didn't open them. "It's me," I whispered. "I'm hallucinating, seeing and smelling and hearing things that my mind just makes up."

And you made up the feathers, I suppose?

"And the flies. All of it."

Again, there was a long stretch of time where there was no talking or whispering. Then the voice said, *When I am strong, you will see.*

Ever so slightly, so gently, I felt breath on my neck, like someone had come closer and was kissing me there lightly. *You also have a scent,* the voice whispered. *Calming. Crushed petals. Rain.*

I relaxed into the cloud of dead leaves and shadows. I couldn't explain why, but I had never felt so comfortable. So at ease. It could have been the medicine, true. But something told me it wasn't. "Do you like my scent, then?" I asked.

Oh yesssssss, the voice whispered.

The breath was on my face, warm and slightly damp. *You really will not open your eyes?* asked the voice.

I shook my head, too tired to say anything else.

Coldness, like someone was holding an ice cube to my lips. But then it warmed, turned into something deep and slick. Something I wasn't sure I should have liked, but I found myself leaning forward, asking for more. My bottom lip was held gently, as if someone's teeth had caught it and was contemplating if they should bite or release me.

"Are you kissing me?" I whispered. My voice was too high, too impossible to keep even.

The movement paused. The wetness disappeared. *Yesssss, I have wanted to for a long time.*

My heart beat loudly in my chest, pounding in my ears and making my head ache.

Too much? whispered the voice. This was followed by a series of murmurs. It sounded like they were all in different languages, whispers and voices mixed into static and white noise.

I nodded despite how much I...*liked* it.

I liked it?

This was something I had made up. This was something that wasn't real. That couldn't be. Yet I wanted more. I wanted more of the cold slickness against my lips. I wanted the hands and arms I couldn't see wrapped around my body, I wanted the voice to speak softly into my ear as I fell asleep.

Did it matter if it was real or not? It made me happy, didn't it? There was so very little that I enjoyed. And besides, I was a creative person with a creative mind. Who was to say that my imagination wasn't just getting carried away because of the years of stress I had gone through? Maybe I had finally reached my threshold and this was my brain's way of protecting itself so I didn't throw myself into a busy intersection of oncoming cars.

"You're a good kisser," I said. "Different."

The hissing slid over my body as another cold, damp embrace of my bottom lip pulled me forward. *I am happy you're pleased.*

I smiled a little. "Is this why you're here?" I asked. "To take advantage of a weak, sick girl?"

There was a hum that vibrated my chest, warmed it from the inside and radiated outward. *Would you like that, my love?* the voice asked. *Would you like to forget who you are for a short time?*

I wanted to open my eyes, to see what or who I was talking

to. I wanted to look into its eyes, if it had them. "God, yes," I whispered back. "You can do that?"

The humming began again. It was like a large vehicle coming down the street; far enough away that I couldn't see it, but close enough that I could feel it underneath my feet. *I can do many things.* The whisper echoed this time, voices layered on top of voices.

I took a deep breath and released it. Along with the air leaving my lungs, I let my thoughts fade away too. I let go of what it meant that I was acting as if this was real. I let go of myself.

Nuzzling my head forward more, the smell of dead leaves only became stronger. "Please," I whispered as the same cold, damp touch landed on my bare shoulder. "I want to disappear."

I can help you with that, my love, said the voice. *Just keep your eyes closed.*

I shut my eyes tighter, as if to prove that I wasn't opening them. "What are you going to do?" I asked in a small voice, one I had never heard myself use before.

Hussshh. It was a command, but gentle. There was almost a laugh behind the whisper. *When I am done, you will finally say my name.*

I shook my head like anyone could see, like I wasn't just talking to myself. Saying the "name" somehow made it even more disturbingly real. If I said it, this became something more than playing make-believe in my own head. The voice would have a consciousness, a past and future. It would be like me or any other person on the street if it had a name, and that was something I was not prepared to deal with.

Maybe, it whispered. *Maaaaayyyybe.*

The blankets around me shifted, lifted off of my front half almost completely. If I opened my eyes I imagined it would be hovering in the air while the other half was still wrapped securely around my back. I didn't dare. I was afraid it would look exactly as I imagined and I was afraid it wouldn't look that way at all.

The hem of my t-shirt lifted next. It wasn't something that I was fully aware of. I was more aware of the leaves in my nose, the softness around me. The sense that there was something in front of me that I couldn't look at. *Are you scared?* the voice whispered.

I swallowed but shook my head. I couldn't be scared of something that wasn't real. I wasn't a child anymore. The touches I felt were only traces. Sketch marks on a blank page. Then the tingling on my lips again, cool and then warm.

My brave little crow, the voice crooned. *Nothing scares you, does it?*

I took in a sharp breath as my shirt came all the way up, over my ribcage, over every private part of me there. It was a swift motion, like a leaf falling from a branch. "I'm doing that," I said to myself. "My hands—"

Tell me, Corbin, the voice whispered, cutting me off. I could feel its breath on my face, the hot prickle of anxiety in my throat. *Where are your hands right now? Can you feel where they are? Why don't you wiggle your fingers and try?*

I wanted to open my eyes, but they were so heavy. It was

easier to keep them closed.

Try. This time, the voice was less than a whisper and more of a low growl. It didn't scare me when I knew that it should have. It was just the sound an animal made. It had no control over how its vocal cords worked.

Slowly, I willed my right index finger to move. I knew where it was: right at my side, but I couldn't move it any more than I could open my eyes. "It's the drugs," I said.

Only partly.

I ignored the voice, reaching out with my mind to where my left hand was. It was under my head, sandwiched between two pillows. I couldn't move any fingers on that one either.

Sssseee? the voice whispered. *I'm doing this to you.* My shirt moved down a few inches, covering my chest at least, leaving my midsection exposed. *I can do many things*, it said. *Many.*

I gulped around a lump in my throat. If this was real, if I was really feeling this, then my brain had really gotten fucked up. I really did need help. If I could hallucinate so well that I could hear and feel things as if they were happening in real time, outside of my body, I was severely screwed.

Feather light touches then. Small, almost imperceptible tickles, moving in small circles on my ribs. It raised goose bumps and made me shiver.

"What are you doing?" I asked in a high pitched whisper. "Are you going to hurt me?" This seemed like a logical question to ask in the dark.

The sensation didn't stop. If anything, it intensified. The

voice, when it spoke next, was full and right next to my ear. *Never,* it said before spinning off into a multitude of whispers. They washed over me like an evening wind: *Neverneverever. Never. Never.*

My body relaxed into the touch of something on my face. It wasn't quite like a hand because there was no hand there. I knew where mine were now and they weren't moving. It was like butterflies, or just plain flies, against my cheek, running along my jaw, across my lower lip. A static electricity that tingled on the verge of pain.

Do you believe yet, Corbin? the whisper said. *Or do you need further convincing?*

"Let me see," I said without hesitation. "Let me see who you are and I'll believe."

The feeling on my face subsided, but resumed on my abdomen. My head was heavy and sunk into the pillow. The blackness behind my eyes spun and pulsed from lighter to dark. *No,* the voice said. *Not yet.*

CHAPTER
ELEVEN

SOMETHING HIT THE WINDOW. A sharp *thunk* punctuating the darkness where I floated.

When I sat up, my neck was sore. It felt like I had slept the entire night in a sitting position with my arms behind my back. But when I opened my eyes, I was still on my side, in the same position I was in when I fell asleep. I stretched my arms over my head and shifted my head from side to side. I blinked a few times, my sinuses aching with each movement. I felt like I had ground my teeth incredibly hard during the night. That was something I hadn't done since I was very small.

My legs were like Jell-o, unstable and untrustworthy. I was afraid when I stood they would collapse under my weight. I had to lean against the bedpost when I crossed the room. I braced my palm against the wall of shelves as I made my way to the window, to where the sound had come from.

It was unbearably hot.

My T-shirt clung to my chest with sweat and I tied my hair up to get if off of my back. My bare legs slicked against one another as I moved forward. Quickly, I threw the window open and let in the air from outside. It was only slightly cooler.

In the flowerbox beneath the window, the one that had not been tended to since I was seven years old, flowers were blooming. They weren't roses. Not daffodils or even dandelions. They weren't any flower I had seen before. Instead of the delicate petals of red or pink wrapping around one another, there were dark blue buds, bursting with yellow and then a blue so dark it looked black. They may have existed somewhere in this world, but not in our yard. Not in our house.

I tried to search for where the sound had come from, but there was nothing I could tell that could have caused it. There were no fallen branches, no animals sitting nearby, not even a ball from some kids playing that may have hit the glass. Just a handful of these strange flowers staring up at me.

I blinked a few times before I pried my shaking hands off of the windowsill. Reaching down into the flowerbox, I picked one of the strange flowers, surprised when the stem came off in my hand and the petals didn't immediately turn to flies or feathers. It was a relief, but only a small one. How had flowers appeared over night? Was Mom planting again? If so, how had I not heard her while I was asleep?

I brought the flower to my nose and inhaled. Instead of smelling like roses, it smelled of fall. Dead leaves and rain. I glanced at the box on my shelf, afraid I would find more inside.

But I placed the flower on my nightstand and abandoned my sweltering room for a cold shower.

I undressed quickly, turning the tap to the temperature of pool water. I made a mental note to check the side effects of my sleeping pills to see if night sweats were something I could look forward to as I slipped the white plastic curtain around me and let the cool water wash down my face. It was like coming up for air after being underground. It was a shock—the freezing cold against steaming hot—but a welcome one. I needed something to break me out of the previous night's stupor and this morning's grogginess. I didn't think about the voice. I didn't think about my hands. Or its, if it had hands.

Not until I grabbed the soap and started scrubbing.

Straining against the torrent of water that created a curtain of hair around my face, I looked down at my feet as I lathered my rag. When I saw my stomach, I had to lean against the wall so I didn't fall over.

But I found I didn't have to. There was something else in the room with me as I gasped in water and sputtered out damp breath.

I have you, the voice said in my ear. *I have you.*

I lurched forward, trying desperately to turn around and see who was holding me. I couldn't see anything around my waist where I felt the strong hold keeping me upright. On my stomach was one word:

Six.

I have you, my love, the voice said yet again. There was the rush of air, the pounding of water against the tiles, my skin, my scalp. It was hot against my face even though I hadn't adjusted the temperature since I stepped inside.

The marks on my abdomen were unlike anything I had seen before. They were in raised pink packages, tied together with blue bruises.

Raising a shaking hand from the wall, I slowly brought it closer to my middle. My fingertips lightly grazed the marks. When it didn't hurt the way a bruise and scratch should, I rubbed. I took soap and water in my washcloth and tried to scrub them away until my skin was red and raw. But the word remained. Six.

My breathing was hard to control and the water only made it that much harder to remain upright. I cut the water, let the remaining drops hit me square in the face as I stared at the ceiling so I wouldn't have to look down. I wanted to turn around. I wanted to see who or what was holding me up. I wanted to prove to myself that I was alone. That I had somehow done this to myself as I slept. Maybe my mind had convinced itself that these words were written and then it was so. Maybe I had multiple personalities and during my black outs I did things like this.

There was one moment of silence. One small, quick, fleeting moment when I didn't hear anything except my ragged breathing, the water that remained in the bottom of the tub draining out.

Do you sssssseeee now?

I squeezed my eyes shut tight. "Can I see you?" I asked with a trembling voice.

Silence.

"Please," I said a little too loudly. I had to take a breath before I continued in a softer voice. "Please let me see you. Just for a second. I need to know for sure."

This is not enough? it whispered.

I didn't know what to say, so I said nothing. I watched as water droplets accumulated on my bare skin and I noticed how I hadn't even gotten around to washing off yesterday's dirt from my hands and arms. My hair was soaked and freezing against my back. Outside, the birds were singing. Inside, Mom was listening to Frank Sinatra and cooking breakfast. How could everything be so normal when inside this small enclosed space, everything in my little chunk of world was turning to dust? It was only a matter of time before things got worse. I just wanted to know what I was dealing with.

Keep your eyes closed until I tell you to open them. The voice was in my ear, taking up any space between me and it.

Oxygen caught in my chest, a bubble of fear I couldn't speak around.

Is that okay? For the first time since it appeared, the voice sounded almost hesitant. Like it needed my approval.

I nodded without opening my eyes.

I felt the warm breath against the back of my cold neck. It made me shiver and wrap my arms around myself. It was as if I hadn't realized I was naked until this very moment. It only seemed logical to reach to my right where my towel was hanging from the shower rod and wrap it around myself. It took away the chill slightly. Only slightly.

There was a chatter of voices then. Whispers on top of whispers. Static. Then, *Turn around, Corbin.*

Inch by inch, I pivoted on one foot until I was facing the opposite direction. I stood there for an immeasurable amount of time. It could have been seconds or minutes. Lifetimes. The low hum of static filled my ears, the scent of dead leaves filled my nose, scratched the back of my throat, tickled my eyelashes.

"Are you still there?" I whispered, immediately feeling stupid, like I had no right to ask such a question.

Yesssssss, the voice echoed back at me.

Then I waited some more. The scent of leaves became stronger, turning to something burned, something that had not quite turned to ash, but was still on fire.

Count to three, the voice whispered, *then open your eyes.*

My head swam. My hands shook even though they were firmly wrapped around myself and holding onto the towel. I took a deep breath and counted quietly to myself. Three small seconds and my eyes opened. I was face to face with who had been speaking to me for the past month.

I saw the face first. The full curve of the bottom lip, the even dip of the cupid's bow in the top lip. The angled jaw, clenched with concern. The hair slicked back and light in color, but not quite blonde. And the eyes. A deep dark blue. When I looked past the face of this creature in front of me, he had no shirt, and water dripped from his broad, pale shoulders. I didn't look past that before I heard the voice again. This time, it was full and in no way could be mistaken for a whisper. *Close your eyes again.*

I regretted that my gaze hadn't traveled back up to his face in time to see his mouth form the words. I wanted to see how they worked. If they moved at all or if I just heard him speak inside my own mind.

There didn't seem to be any other option than to tightly close my eyes. It took me a few moments to realize there were tears trickling down my cheeks.

Tingling against my lips. The feather light touch of tiny pin pricks on the skin of my face. *Do you believe now, Corbin?* The voice was back to a whisper.

I felt my forehead crease as my eyebrows came together so I could hold in all of the sobs. I nodded.

You can see me any time you like soon, it said, coming from behind me again, like it had changed positions in case I happened to open my eyes and saw something I wasn't meant to see. *I need to gather my strength first.*

Although I believed I had made this thing real, I still knew it was only inside my head. This whole person—the face, the eyes, and body—hadn't come from anywhere except me. My imagination, insecurities, and fears.

Without opening my eyes, I shifted the shower curtain open and stepped out into the warm bathroom, sliding the curtain around me. I wrapped the towel around myself even tighter as I left the bathroom and closed the door. I didn't open my eyes until I was halfway down the hall, when my knees gave out and I fell on the carpet, next to packed winter clothes in big plastic storage crates and miscellaneous books and magazines.

The smell of dust filled my nostrils as I inhaled the fibers of the carpet that probably hadn't been vacuumed in more than six months. It didn't matter. *I* didn't matter. All that mattered was that I calmed down enough to face my mother. My mother, who had been doing so much better on her new meds, the one who I had finally convinced that I was *completely* fine and that she had nothing to worry about. How was I supposed to tell her about this? How would I even begin?

"Corbin?" she called from the kitchen. "Honey, are you alright?" she asked. "Was that you, sweetie?"

I sniffed and got to my feet. "Yeah!" I called back. "Just tripped over a book. I'm fine." I retreated back into my room and dressed quickly, refusing to look out the window at the strange flowers, and I didn't look at the bookshelf where the box with the intricate metalwork was. I didn't look to my stained sheets or the few feathers that no doubt lay beneath the comforter. I simply dressed in shorts and a tank top, grabbed my bag, and left to join Mom for breakfast.

She was already sitting at the table when I entered the kitchen, reading the newspaper and eating bacon and eggs. There was a plate with a bowl over the top of it for me sitting across from her. The entire table was also cleared off for us. Out of all the things that had been happening recently, this was one thing I had not seen coming. "Wow," I said. "The table looks great, Mom."

She looked up from the paper and smiled sweetly. The rollers in her hair looked tight, but her expression was easy and happy. "Thank you, sweetie," she said. "I'm having a friend over for coffee later so I wanted us to have somewhere to sit."

I wiggled my eyebrows at her, a frail attempt to joke when inside, all of my organs were systematically shutting down. Starting with my brain. "A friend, eh?" I said. "Anyone I know?"

I picked up my fork and ate around the well done brown parts of my scrambled eggs. I took a sip of orange juice between bites so I could wash it all down without choking.

Mom simply shrugged. "It's just been a while since anyone's come to visit," she said. "It'll be nice to have a friend here for a change."

"Sure," I said, noticing the dull throb in my side where I had tried to scrub off the word. "What time are they getting here?" I asked. "I'd love to meet them, but I'm supposed to spend the day with Jordan."

Mom waved a dismissive hand. "Oh don't bother yourself," she said. "Go have fun. There will be plenty of time for you to meet my friends."

"Using the plural form of the word now, are we?" I joked again.

We both knew that when Mom was on bad meds or no meds at all, she didn't want to be around anyone. Not even me, the one person in this world she loved and trusted more than anyone else. This was just another sign that she really was doing better, that the doctors really had helped this time. If there was hope for her, maybe there was some for me too. But in order to reach that goal, I had to ask for help first. And asking for help would reveal everything. To her and everyone else I knew. I wasn't ready to be that person. Another of the Greene women to lose their shit.

That wasn't me.

Not yet.

MY FINGERS WERE SHAKING AS I put the key in the ignition. I glanced at my face in the rearview mirror and saw that my eyes were puffy and rimmed in dark circles. Left over makeup I hadn't the chance to wash away because of my interrupted shower. I turned on the air full blast, wishing I could stop sweating as I reached into my bag for my sketchbook.

I flipped the few pages. Past the self-portraits and figure studies. Past the nudes of Jordan and the few of myself. Past the ink-blot drawings of the dragon fly creature I couldn't quite get right.

There it was.

The face I had drawn without looking.

The same one that had stared back at me only minutes ago.

I brought a trembling hand to my lip to keep myself from screaming.

Putting the car in reverse, I knew where I had to go. It didn't matter what I wanted. If I didn't want to end up like Mom, I had to stop thinking like her. I had to stop repeating her mistakes.

What are you intending to do, Corbin? the voice echoed from somewhere in the back of my head.

Waiting until I was farther from the house, I cranked the stereo as loud as I could as I sped down the street and onto the freeway. I had been there so many times over the years that I knew how to get there like the map was implanted in my brain, casting the directions in front of me.

Corbin. The voice was deeper now, but I could barely hear it over the screaming guitar solo of some classic rock song. *Think about what you are about to do.*

I laughed to myself as I turned off on the exit. "I've never been surer about something," I said. "I don't need to think. Thinking is what got me here."

Suddenly, the radio cut off, turning into a vague mechanical sound and then static white noise. When the voice came next, it was directly through the speakers.

"Please, my love," the voice practically boomed. I lowered the dial, not quite strong enough to turn the sound off. "They will hurt you. They will not understand."

I switched on my blinker as I stopped at the intersection. "If you're real, you'll have nothing to worry about," I said in a quiet voice. "Right?"

More static. More mechanical nothingness, metal on metal, sound waves against sound waves, never quite locking together in order to form a clear picture of the words they were trying to say.

The light turned green. I made the left turn onto the street I knew by heart. There was a large willow right on the corner. An old church covered in ivy a few houses down. Across the street from that, there was a school where children played outside in blue and white plaid uniforms and shiny new shoes. My head spun but I was only going twenty miles an hour. I had to clench my fingers around the steering wheel so I wouldn't let go. So I wouldn't turn around. So I wouldn't reach into my bag and get my phone so I could call someone to come get me, tell me I was okay and that I didn't need to do this.

When I was finally in front of the large, brown brick building with its many windows looking out, the shady courtyard where the maple leaves were bright green and blinding, I couldn't take the sound of static anymore. It was like spider webs forming in my mind, sticking from fold to fold until it was nothing but a jumbled ball of thin, translucent white yarn.

The sign for Cedar Ridge claimed: *Recovery Begins Here.*

I hoped so.

"*I am terrified by this dark thing that sleeps within me.*"

—SYLVIA PLATH

PART TWO:

BURNING CEDAR

CHAPTER
TWELVE

IT'S AMAZING WHAT WE TAKE for granted on a daily basis. If you're hungry, you either make something or pay someone else to do it for you. If you're lonely, there are millions of people on the planet that are willing to interact with you, even if they're just holding the door for you at the bank. If you want to go to the bathroom, you excuse yourself and do your business. If you want to sleep, you sleep. If you want to be left alone, you sit at home and watch Netflix until there are no more episodes of *The X-files* left.

Here, it was different.

You had to ask permission for everything. You had to *earn* everything. If you had to pee, someone followed you and waited outside the door. If you wanted to go by yourself, you needed enough points to warrant that trip alone. And even then, you had to sign in and out and were timed. You had a choice if you wanted to wake up at six with everyone, if you wanted to eat, if you wanted to join the rest of the group as they talked, but if you chose not to go, it was noted. Highlighted and underlined and never missed.

I had been at Cedar Ridge for a little over three days. When I showed up, they took my belongings and shoved them in a locker behind the nurses' desk. When I signed in, they informed me of my rights. How I was signing them away until I was well. My sneakers were replaced with flat, uncomfortable slippers and they made my feet stiff as I followed one of the orderlies to the room I would be sharing with someone I had never met. I still wasn't sure that I had made the right decision.

"Is there anyone who should know you're here?" the man who initially evaluated me asked. We were in a rec room by ourselves and he had explained everyone had gone to various activities. I sat in an orange plastic chair and watched as he filled out sheet after sheet of paper.

"My mom," I said with as little emotion as possible. If I let it in now, it would completely spill out of me and there would be no way to stop it.

I gave him her number and he handed me off to someone else, a nurse in pink scrubs who took blood from my arm and tested it for drugs.

Then I was given some general medication. Something for anxiety. Something to knock me out. I slept for eight hours straight.

All of the things happening at once made my head spin. One minute I was completely in control of my life—well, at least on the outside. Now I had given all of that control to complete strangers, trusting them to make everything better. Make me normal again.

Out of all the things to change that day, one was the most unexpected: the voice had not spoken. Not once. Not while I was checking in or talking to the medical doctors or giving my family history or explaining why I was there. It was so quiet that I found myself questioning why I had actually come. Had I simply imagined everything? Was I overreacting? Did I really have to check into an inpatient place when all I had to do was talk to a counselor once a week and go about my business the rest of the six days?

I couldn't be sure.

But by the third day, the voice came back to me the moment I woke up. It whispered in my ear as I showered with the other girls, nurses standing in the wings so none of us tried anything funny or dangerous. It said things like how we would get out. How I had made a mistake but that it understood why. It didn't blame me for being afraid. It only wanted to show me how real it was. It only wanted me to see.

"You gonna eat that?"

I blinked a few times. Whatever they had me on made my movements slow and my brain even slower. It took a long time to connect words to sentences and make those sentences cohesive enough to make sense. I stared down at the spongy yellow disk that was supposed to be scrambled eggs in the middle of my styrofoam tray and shook my head.

The girl sitting across from me took her spork and speared it with the dull prongs, sliding the already cold material onto her own tray. She told me her name when she sat down, but I had already forgotten. Her hair hung limply in her face and her ears stuck out too far from her head. She had overgrown, thick, dark eyebrows and whenever she spoke, I saw just how shiny, translucent, and damaged her teeth were. Someone had told me she was bulimic, but gossip spread in this place just as badly as it had in high school. I didn't believe anything until the person in question admitted to it.

She scarfed down the food, chugging her miniature chocolate milk carton to wash it down. I picked at the mixed fruit cup sitting in one of the square imprints of my tray, only eating the single cherry off of it before I decided I wasn't hungry. I knew there were most likely people watching. There always were. And if they saw me push food away long enough, they'd be less inclined to release me. I was so nauseous from the sleeping pills they switched me to—they were different than the ones I had been taking for the past few weeks—that I didn't care.

I wrapped my robe around myself tighter, my fingers heavy, like they were made out of slugs and couldn't grasp anything.

"Whoa," the girl sitting across from me said. "They really fucked you up, huh?"

It took my eyes a long time to meet her face again, but when they did, I gave her a single, slow nod.

Sitting in the cafeteria with a bunch of strangers reminded me of school—minus everyone wearing pajamas. I was a lonely child, but I never really realized it until someone pointed it out to me. Teachers would ask why I was sitting alone; kids steered clear of me when I didn't offer conversation. As a kid, I never thought twice about it. I would much rather draw in my notebook while eating my Elio's pizza than have to speak to anyone. Real people had too many variables. If I drew them, I didn't have to worry about what they thought, how we could relate, or if they knew about my mother. As I grew older and entered middle school, I avoided the lunchroom altogether, spending most of my time in the art studio organizing paint or working on my own projects.

But people knew. No one talked to me because I was the kid who stared at her feet when she walked. I was the one with the sunken in eyes from not sleeping because I worried about when mom would come home or when she would go away. I wouldn't say I was bullied exactly. Bullies called you names, wrote things on your locker, threw eggs at your house on Halloween. None of that ever happened to me. Instead of being insulted, I was ignored. Like I wasn't even part of the school, like I didn't even exist.

When I got into college, I thought I had left it all behind, but everyone has a shadow. You can't just wake up one day unattached to it.

A bell rang from an intercom somewhere above us, but I could only barely hear it. I couldn't move, and I could barely see anything besides the blur of bodies throwing out their trays and heading off in different directions to their next activity.

"Yo, this girl's freaking!" I heard the girl in front of me say, and momentarily, my vision cleared. I could see her standing, her stringy hair swaying in her face as she turned her head toward a man in green scrubs coming my way.

"Thanks, Patricia," he said to her as he sat down next to me and gently grabbed hold of my elbow. "You can head to group now."

"You guys need to get your shit together," she said to no one in particular. "Drugging us like we're some kind of show dogs for your therapists..." She went on, but it was mostly incoherent chatter and I could barely hear it over the voice inside of my own head.

They are going to take you away if you don't stand up.

I didn't want to listen, but the voice was right. I tried to stand, but there was a strong hand on my shoulder, keeping me still. "What's your name?" the man in scrubs asked, but the words echoed.

Slowly, I turned my head and could see him clearly for a few moments. He had a round face and dark, closely clipped hair. His cheeks were red, but not because he was blushing. They just looked perpetually pink.

"Corbin," I whispered, and even that came out slurred.

"Corbin," he said. "Are you feeling alright?"

I shook my head, the world spinning out of focus once more.

That girl was right, said the voice. *They give you drugs to keep you quiet. To prove they're helping you.*

I shook my head again. I didn't want to listen to this right now—I came here for help. I knew what I was doing.

I didn't notice that the guy had called over a nurse in pink scrubs until she was right in front of me, flipping through a chart on a cheery blue clipboard. "Yes," she said. "Corbin Greene." She proceeded to tell the first intern of all the medication they had me on, horing in on a specific one I could not hear completely or pronounce. "That one must be too strong," she said simply. "We'll readjust it for your night meds, alright?"

It occurred to me that she might have been speaking to me the entire time, but I only realize it now. I nodded, my brain sloshing inside my skull.

"I'll excuse you from activities today as well," she said. "Let you sleep it off."

I saw her lips move more than anything.

That will give us more time together, my love. The voice was in front of me instead, blocking out whatever else the lady was saying.

I didn't want to go to sleep. I didn't want to give this thing—whatever it was inside of me—a chance to go walking again.

The nurse left. I could hear her tennis shoes squeaking on the linoleum. The man in green scrubs stood, holding out his hand for me to take. When I didn't move, he wrapped a strong arm around my shoulder and helped me up.

"Nothing to be afraid of, Corbin," he said gently as we made our way slowly into the hall. His shoes thudded against the floor and mine scuffed. "My name is Syd, by the way. I'm the new lunch room monitor."

I shrugged. That was the only answer I could give him.

"You'll feel better after a nap," he said distantly, like I was on the bottom level of a ladder and he was at the top, waiting for me to climb.

We shuffled as one unit into my shared room. We didn't have a door, but they did allow us thick curtains to give us some sense of privacy and block out the bright lights from the nurses' station. My roommate's bed was neatly made (I still hadn't met her because she was always awake and asleep before me) and mine was a mass of balled up blankets, the sheet hanging off. He sat me in the wooden desk chair as he made it for me.

"You know," he said, fluffing a pillow he picked up from the floor, "if you don't make your bed, you can't earn points."

I blinked slowly, my eyelids too tired to pick up the pace or take in anything besides his strong, sure hands against the worn yellow cotton of my borrowed blankets.

The whispers were still buzzing around my head like flies, but I couldn't make them out right now either. At least there was a plus side to being fucked out of my mind.

When he was finished, he stood upright and came back to me, helping me up the same way he did before with his arm around my shoulders. I sat on the bed with shaky legs, and he helped me cover myself with the blankets. As my head settled into the pillow, he noted the small nightlight I had requested on my first night here and he switched it on. He smiled reassuringly at me as I brought the covers up to my chin and he turned out the light, leaving me in the dark except for a dull yellow glow that casted shadows on the wall.

CHAPTER
THIRTEEN

A TAP ON THE WINDOW. Something that was too much like a tree branch to really draw any attention. Then it got louder. I shoved the pillow over my head, sinking its weight into the cool fabric and throwing the covers over my head for extra good measure. I almost forgot where I was until I felt the rough fabric of the blanket that wasn't mine. I tried to open my eyes, but I didn't care enough to exert the amount of energy it took. Instead, I rolled over, sinking deeper into the darkness surrounding me.

I knew somehow that I had slept through all the daily activities, through group therapy and arts and crafts and TV hour. I knew it was past lights out and I found myself not caring that it would all be monitored. I could stay in this room, in this bed forever. Somewhere between sleeping and waking, between my body and muddy, thick mind, I heard the voice. I couldn't understand what it said, but it was a gentle, almost cooing sound, like one a mother would use on a child who had woken in the middle of the night from a bad dream. But they were down the hall and too far away to offer me anything.

The blanket shifted and I couldn't see because my eyes were closed; the blankets and pillow still covered my head. A moment of quiet, then the mattress dipped in next to me, in front of me. My heart pounded in my head, my throat. A second later, the pillow slid from my head, but I couldn't tell if it was my own doing. My head was too heavy; my thoughts were too clogged to get one solitary explanation through.

Hush now, the voice whispered. It was right next to my ear, right next to me. *I'll show you.*

Yes. Show me. Show me how to be insane. Show me how to be just like my mother. I kept my eyes completely closed.

Corbin, said the voice. As much as I hated to admit it, I liked the sound of my name in its tone. I liked how it hit me deep. It was the sound of sand being blown by the sea on a windy day. It was the feeling of fingers in your hair as you fell asleep, tangled limbs after a closely spent night. Softness and hardness of an intimate touch, one that couldn't have possibly been delivered by anyone or anything else.

"Yes?" I hadn't realized I said the word out loud until my hot breath was bouncing back at me against the covers. I was afraid my roommate would hear, but her heavy snoring reassured me.

So you are with me, it whispered. Each word caressed my face, sent warm shivers through my skin and into the bone.

I opened my mouth to say something else, but I couldn't think of anything; I doubted I would even be able to get the words past my teeth.

Hushhhhhh, said the voice. I felt something slightly cold, yet not completely solid against my waist. It wasn't enough to make me shiver. It wasn't anything that woke me further from the drugs. My shirt slipped upward, past my belly button before it stopped.

I inhaled sharply and turned over onto my back, convinced that I was half-dreaming and if I switched positions, the dream would change just as easily.

A few moments of silence. A few moments of the tapping on the glass, the rustle of the wind outside as the rain pelted the roof. It lulled me back into comfort, back into darkness.

My little crow, crooned the voice. Again, right in my ear, right in front of my face. It made the blackness behind my eyelids shake, sprout leaves and take root. *My precious petal.*

I was almost unaware of the sheet moving off of me, the blankets shifting until I heard them rumple into a careless pile on the floor. My face became warm, the smell of damp dirt in my nostrils, the sound of static electricity zipping through my brain, setting off synapses to synapses.

"What are you doing?" I whispered. But my voice sounded so far away, like I was standing on top of a very high tower and trying to make my words heard to people down below.

I felt my hair being moved from my forehead, then a small, sweet amount of pressure applied there. *Kissing you, my love.*

I liked the gesture. It overrode any logic, any sense of self I could bring forth from the darkness.

"Why do you only kiss me at night?" I whispered.

Another small peck, warm and then cool against my cheek. *I am strongest at this hour.* The words slithered around my skin, crawled to the back of my skull like some creature that had suddenly sprouted legs. *And you are most open to me.*

"Open?" I asked, my head swimming with medication, my eyes glued shut, my body heavy with sleep that had yet to come.

I felt the slight breath of an amused, silent laugh. *Yesssss,* the voice whispered. *Open, my crow.*

I opened my eyes, but I was only met with darkness. I knew that it was all in my head as the dim room spun around me, but I didn't care. I didn't want to think about it or what it meant. It was easier to pretend. If I was the only one who knew, I was the only one who knew the truth. I couldn't be losing my mind if I was so in control of it.

"Open," I repeated, more content with the word.

Yesssssss.

My head felt sewn to the mattress, my limbs glued in place. I tried opening my eyes after blinking, but that was no use. It was amazing how much the world could spin when I couldn't see any of it.

Be still, said the voice.

That was strange. By the light pink color behind my eyelids, I could tell that it was morning. The sun was out. A second ago it was dark.

"Why..." was all I could get out of my mouth. The rest of the question turned to ash on my tongue.

You can't see me yet, my love, said the voice. It was a deep, throaty sound. Something that came from within someone's chest. *I am not fully formed.*

The back of my skull sunk into the mattress. I took a deep breath and tried to speak again.

"What do you look like?" I asked again.

Now?

I nodded.

A small laugh, but it was a fuller sound than I had heard come from it before. *I am more...solid now,* said the voice. *But not as much as I would like. Not in the right order.*

I snorted, my mind wandering. "So you have a foot on your head or something?"

Another short laugh. *No, my love,* he said. It was a "he." It sounded positively male. *What I look like now is nothing you have seen before. Nothing I want you to see.*

"Why?"

There was a pause. I could still smell the burned leaves. The slight scent of dirt and dried grass against my pillow. *I want you,* it said. *You would not like this form.*

I sighed heavily. More evading questions. More proof this was nothing more than something my mind cooked up to get me through some rough times.

My hair was lifted from the back of my neck. "Are you a boy ghost or a girl ghost?" I asked. I couldn't help what I said, my mind sloshing inside my skull.

There was cool breath against my face and warmth in the pit

of my stomach that I wasn't sure was fear or anticipation. *I am no ghost.*

I cleared my throat. "Then what are you?"

Unseen fingers ran through my hair, lingered at my face. *You are not ready to know.* The sentence echoed around me, sent shivers through the back of my head and around my eye sockets. It sounded like something someone's mind would make up. I wasn't surprised.

"So..." I said. "Boy or girl?"

I am neither, it said. *I am both.* There was a pause, one that was long enough to notice the indentation in the bed growing, like someone was merely leaning, testing out the waters before they had put their full weight down and decided to get comfortable. *Although when I am strong enough, I am not sure which form I shall take.*

My head was buzzing, swimming with the scent of burned leaves and the feeling of my nose going chilled, like I had been outside in winter without a hat. "Why are you so cold?"

I wanted to open my eyes, but I didn't. I was more afraid that we wouldn't be talking anymore if I did and I didn't want the voice to leave me. Not now.

I am weak, it said. *I need more to be...more.*

"To be warm?" I asked. "To be a boy or girl?"

Precissssssely. The voice snaked around me, squeezing slightly around my arms and legs just enough to make me feel secure.

"H—" I paused, unsure of what I wanted to ask next or whether I even wanted to know anything else. "How will you do that?"

Shhhhh. It was like a cool breeze on a hot summer day around my face. I smelled flowers—roses. The one small window in our room was closed. I was sure of it. There was no way the smell could come from anywhere else but from somewhere inside. *You ask too much*, it whispered. *You expect everything to have an answer.*

There was a gentle caress of my hand, my index finger on top of the blanket. "How can you touch me?" I asked.

There was just a light, airy chuckle. I had only proven the voice right.

I laughed softly too, suddenly aware of the ridiculousness of the whole thing. Aware that it would probably get more absurd but not caring. "Could you kiss me again?" I asked.

There wasn't another word. Just the small pins and needles dancing on my lower lip. The curl of my mouth as I smiled at the sensation.

Another kiss, this time deeper, the coolness of an unseen tongue that belonged to no body to speak of. If this was my imagination, I had a really good one. If this was something else, I sensed I was only beginning to cause myself more problems.

The rain outside continued to assault the side of the building, coming down in sheet after sheet and hitting the glass of our tiny window. My chest swelled as I gasped for air, but not in an uncomfortable way. My cheeks were hot, my skin no doubt flushed. I broke away and turned my head to the side, hoping this was enough of a signal to show that I needed a breather, though I wasn't sure who I was trying to get the message across to.

Let me be part of you, the voice whispered. *Let me help you. Make you better. Is that not what you want?*

The slight pressure of sleep was upon me, like someone had stretched a blanket over my skin and made sure that not one inch was uncovered. "Yes," I whispered.

I expected it to kiss me more, something else to happen; maybe the kissing to travel to somewhere else in my body. Maybe another swarm of flies would come clinking against the window. I wasn't sure of what to expect.

Then tell me what my name is, it whispered. *You know it.*

I shook my head. I wasn't sure what the big deal was in saying it out loud, but I knew deep down that saying it only made the whole situation real.

Yessssss, the voice said, wrapping around my face. *It is real, my little crow*, it said. *Make me real.*

My mouth was so dry and I was finding it difficult to swallow. "Is that why you're here?" I asked against my closed eyelids.

I need you, it whispered. *You need me.*

"But I don't," I said a little too loudly, hoping no one was awake yet to hear.

None of that, the voice said in a gentle way, like it was telling a child to calm down, there would be ice cream later. *Just tell me my name and we will both get what we want.*

"You'll leave me alone?" I asked.

That same light laugh. *I never said that*, it said. *And that is not what you truly want.*

I squeezed my eyes shut tighter. Maybe it was right. If I made something up, I could control it in some way, right? So if I did as it asked, maybe it wouldn't be so bad. "Okay," I said. "Six."

Sixxxxx, it said *Yesssss*. My bottom lip tingled as invisible teeth grazed the thin delicate skin there. *My name tastes beautiful on your lips.*

I let out a breath as the gesture repeated itself, as the blankets dipped in near my legs, near my head. I felt a weight on my thighs, my wrists. It was like someone was sitting on top of me, and I knew if I tried to move, I wouldn't be able to.

Are you sssscared?

I shook my head even though I could hear my heart pounding in my ears, my breath sticking to my lungs.

Yessss, you are.

"Okay," I said. "I am."

A small laugh, then, *You are mine now.*

"But...you're not real." My voice came out small and choked. I hadn't realized how badly I wanted this whole game of pretend to be reality until I said those words. I had said them many times before, but somehow, now that he was here, more solid, more real, I wanted nothing more than for it all to be true.

I heard the sheets move next to me before I felt them shift against my skin.

There was something warm against my face, trailing down my jaw and resting on my throat. I moved my head backwards, finding I wanted to allow it more access to that vulnerable place where I could be held or restrained.

A small, amused breath warmed the skin around my throat.

It was soft. I couldn't imagine any human hand ever being so soft, yet so firm, giving me the thought that at any moment it could snap me in half, but had the control not to.

Was everything just a dream then, little crow? I felt the breath on my neck, the warm, wet feel of something against my ear. A gentle tug, some form of teeth, but sharper against my earlobe. *Or was that only your mind?* he asked directly into my ear, like the closer the question was to my brain, the closer I became to believing the facts it was telling me.

I shook my head.

Yesssssss, it said. *Tell me how you imagined everything*, it said gently, cooing, the sound of someone who knew the truth but let me have my version of it for far too long.

"You're not real," I whispered. "You can't be. This doesn't happen."

You are quite right, it said against my hair. I felt pins and needles against my lips, the pressure on my throat squeezing slightly. Enough to make my pulse speed up, but not enough to choke off my breathing completely. *These things do not happen.*

"Then..." I tried opening my eyes again, convinced that if I could, I would be met with nothing. No shadows in the rising light of morning, no person sitting next to me in bed. But I couldn't. I couldn't move. I couldn't open my eyes or make it all stop. I was paralyzed from the head down. Hearing and feeling everything, but unable to make it come to a halt. "Why is this happening?" I asked.

I was suddenly afraid. Nothing up until this point had

scared me. Not the voice, the bugs, the sounds late at night. Not the chorus of unfamiliar whispers in the dark as I tried to sleep. Not even the sensation of being touched, kissed in the most private of places. I always held onto the hope that these things only happened in the dark. These things were only made of dreams and fantasies, nothing more. Now that this was happening in the daylight, in a mental hospital, where anyone could see—now that I felt and heard the things only reserved for night time, I was terrified. My pulse quickened. My stomach flipped and a sour taste rose to the back of my throat. I was crazy. I really was. Normal people didn't see and hear things in the middle of the day, when the sun was shining and the birds were chirping and children were playing outside. That didn't happen. It was only reserved for the dark, when they could reasonably remember what had happened, but with distance. With the clarity of morning, these things were dreams. Things like that didn't happen in the day.

Shhhhhh, said the voice. *Do not be sssscared.* I felt the soft and gentle touch of a hand against my cheek, but it wasn't solid. It was only a shadow. The grip on my throat loosened until I didn't feel it at all. *Do not fear me, my love. I would never harm you.*

I let out a shaking breath, my lungs feeling wet and tight, like they were about to burst. I didn't want to cry. I really didn't. But a few hot tears slipped out between my closed eyes. I couldn't stop them.

Shhhhh, it repeated, but it did nothing to comfort me. *Don't be afraid.*

The shadow of a touch made itself even more known, pressing into me on all sides. It was on top of me, next to me, all around. *Shhhh*, now the voice was a whisper. He had suddenly become less solid, more of what I was used to and I didn't know why, but it quieted my heart, made the tears stop falling. I could breathe again.

I relaxed into the mattress, sniffling the rest of the tears away.

There, it whispered. *That's better.*

I took a deep breath. "I'm sorry." I didn't know why, but I felt like I should be apologizing. I didn't want him to go away. I realized that with almost the same terror as all of this happening. I didn't want him to leave me alone in my world, where day by day, things began to make less and less sense.

Hush now, it said. *The rest will be awake and taking you to breakfast soon.* It had curled itself around me and the rest of my body began to tingle with warmth. Now instead of trying to move, open my eyes, I didn't want to. I wanted to stay completely still.

Sleep, it whispered.

"Don't go," I said, surprising myself with how much I wanted this request. "Please stay with me."

I felt the feathery touch, the one I was used to, against my cheek, my lips, in my hair. All the while, the smell of leaves filled me completely. The blankets moved around me again, this time, tucking themselves in around my body, the fabric resting under my chin. It suddenly became darker in the room, and I could hear a distant rumble of thunder somewhere outside. It was going to rain again and I wanted nothing more.

Always, the voice whispered. *Always.*

CHAPTER
FOURTEEN

I HAD BEEN AT CEDAR Ridge for four days and it was only now that they were assigning me a psychologist. I was exhausted from the night before, and although they had "adjusted" my meds so I wasn't a complete zombie, I couldn't shake the fog that still settled all around me.

An aid brought me to a row of shiny white doors where she led me inside to a long, dark, fake wood table. She instructed me to sit in yet another uncomfortable plastic chair—this one blue—and informed me that the doctor would be in shortly.

It was strange, as far as offices went. There was a camera hanging in the ceiling, for one. There were the requisite important-looking bookshelves lining the walls, thick, scholastic books stacked there. No leather chair for me to lie out on, no rolling desk chair for him to sit in either. Just the bookshelves, table, and a small chest in the corner that held an electric tea kettle and mugs. The walls were painted a stark white like the rest of the place, but here and there I saw frames that held diplomas, some drawings that children had made him. It was the most colorful place in Cedar Ridge, and that was saying something.

A middle aged man walked in. "Hello, Corbin," he said, taking a seat across from me. "My name is Doctor Howard. I'm going to be your psychologist while you stay here."

"I thought Doctor Marge was my psychologist." I was introduced to her on the first day.

He set down two styrofoam cups on the table as he rested his briefcase on the floor by his chair. I eyed the steaming cup in front of me, the white mist rising like smoke from a burning building.

"She's the group therapist," Doctor Howard said as he opened his briefcase and produced a manila folder. He reached into his faded brown shirt pocket and clicked open a pen. It was one that people stole from banks when they were writing their checks or depositing money into their accounts. I could see the logo sticking out between his fingers. "I'm your personal therapist. For one on ones," he clarified.

I played with the sleeve of my sweatshirt around my wrist, picking the frayed fabric apart. "So you're here to talk to me about what's wrong with me."

He smiled to himself under his thick framed glasses. "I'm here to talk about whatever you want to talk about." He took a sip from his styrofoam cup. I envied him, the warmth he must have gotten out of it.

"Why is it so cold in here?" I asked.

Doctor Howard set his cup down and smiled knowingly. "They crank the heat in the winter and blast the A/C in the summer," he said. "It's never comfortable."

Indeed, the voice whispered.

I couldn't help the smile that spread on my face.

"Would you like some coffee?" he asked, indicating the untouched cup in front of me, pushing it forward slightly. "Or tea? We have tea too."

I blinked a few times, letting my mind catch up. "Tea would be great."

He tapped the table a few times as he stood and turned to an electric tea kettle. He opened a drawer in the cabinet and took out a wooden box that made my chest ache. I missed my box. I wanted it with me. I felt like the farther away I was from it, the farther away I was from home.

Doctor Howard produced an individually wrapped tea bag from the box before setting in on his desk. I watched his hands as he tore open the packet and placed it into a mug he grabbed from the cabinet. When the water was hot enough, he poured it into the cup and slid it over to me as he sat back down.

"Is something wrong?" he asked.

I hadn't noticed that my eyes had lingered on the box of teabags. I hadn't noticed that he was watching my every move. I should have known better. There was always someone watching.

"Just tired," I said, wrapping my hands around the cup as he handed it to me and averting my eyes from the box he left out. From the smell of it, the tea was chamomile. Not the caffeine the coffee would allow, but I didn't want the bitterness in my mouth—this morning's pills had already given me enough. At least it was warm.

Doctor Howard picked up his pen again; he hadn't taken his eyes off of me so I stared at the table. "I understand," he said. "Is there something wrong with my tea chest?"

The question was absurd, but this was an absurd situation. "No," I said. "Not at all."

He nodded to himself and scribbled something down. The paper was right in front of me as he wrote, but his handwriting was so tiny and dark that I couldn't make out what it said.

"Why don't you tell me why you checked yourself in," he said as he folded his hands together in front of him.

He's trying to show you he doesn't need to write anything down, the voice whispered.

I took a deep breath and prayed the voice would stop. I didn't want these people to keep me longer than I wanted to be here. I just wanted to know what was wrong.

"I've been seeing things," I said.

"Like what?"

"Shadows, stains, bugs..." I didn't mention the face.

He reached into his briefcase on the floor again and took out my sketchpad. My heart sunk. I just had to bring it in with me when I checked in, didn't I?

"May I?" he asked, gesturing toward the book.

I took a sip of my tea. It was too strong and tasted like grass. "You haven't already looked at it?"

Doctor Howard shook his head. "I thought I would leave it up to you."

He wants you to trust him, whispered the voice.

I brought my hand up and scratched the side of my head, blocking my left ear momentarily with my wrist. I knew it wouldn't stop the voice, but it made me feel more in control.

"Sure," I said.

The sound of thick paper turning the air around us was all I heard for a while, and I was grateful.

"You're an artist, then?" he asked as he closed the book, setting it to his side, just far enough away that I wouldn't be able to reach across the table to retrieve it.

I shrugged. "I like to draw and paint," I said. "I'm going to art school."

He folded his hands together once more. "You must be very creative then."

I shrugged.

Doctor Howard smiled down at the closed book. "Are you hearing things as well?"

I nodded. "A voice."

"Only one?" He asked it so conversationally. It made my pulse beat rapidly in my ears. These things shouldn't be spoken out loud.

"Sometimes it sounds like...echoing," I said. "But I think it's the same voice."

"And what does the voice say?"

I took another sip from my cup in the hopes that the strong

herbal taste would clear my throat from whatever was preventing me from speaking. I waited for a response from the voice, but there was none.

'Sometimes it's just whispers I can't understand,' I said slowly. "Other times..."

"Does it tell you to do bad things?" he asked. "Does it tell you negative things about yourself?"

I shook my head. "Never," I said. "If anything...it's...nice to me."

My eyes traveled from the table to his face and he was writing something down in his dark, small cursive. "What kind of nice things does it say?" he asked.

I shrugged. "Nothing specific, really. Just...it isn't mean to me or anything."

He nodded like he knew how uncomfortable I was getting and he folded his hands back on top of his paperwork. "When do you usually see things?" he asked. "Is it when the voice is there or when it's gone?"

"Sometimes when the voice is there and sometimes when it's not."

"Okay," he said to himself. "And this voice," he said, "is it male or female? Is it the same voice you hear when say, you're reading to yourself or thinking?"

I shook my head. "I'm not sure," I said. "Mostly I think..." I stared at the cup in my hands. It was doing nothing to warm me up. I kept staring as I thought back to the conversation I had with the voice only the night before. "I think the voice is male."

Interesting. It sounded amused.

Doctor Howard nodded to himself, picked up his stolen bank pen, and scribbled something else down. "What about your family life?" he asked in attempt to change the subject. Or at least that's what he wanted me to think. Everything here was connected.

'It's just me and my mom," I said simply, like we could just leave it at that. I knew there was no such hope.

"Ah yes," he said, flipping over a page or two. "Susan Greene?"

I nodded. "That's her, alright."

His eyes scanned over the page in front of him. He read her multiple diagnoses like he was reading himself a recipe, one hand in the book keeping it open, one hand grabbing his coffee as he drank. "Schizophrenia, Borderline Personality Disorder, and OCD."

"To name a few," I tried to joke. "But she doesn't have OCD; she's a hoarder."

Doctor Howard closed that file and looked at me in a friendly way. "Believe it or not, hoarding is a type of OCD. Something left over from our animalistic instincts that tells us to gather things around us for safety."

I smiled sheepishly. I didn't really care about this information, only if it was connected to me. "Do you think..." I said in a small voice. "Do you think that maybe I have what she has?"

He glanced at her history again and then back at me, giving me the same friendly smile before he folded his friendly hands in his lap. "Tell you what," he said. "I'm going to start you on new medicine." He took out a small pad from his shirt pocket and scribbled my fate down on a clean sheet. "It'll help with the auditory and visual hallucinations," he explained. "You'll start on it tonight and if you're better by your two week stay, we'll do this more as an out-patient relationship."

I took a sip from my lukewarm cup just so I had something to do. "It'll help?" I asked.

Nothing can stop me, my love, the voice whispered, but it was weak. *Try as you might.*

"It should," he said, finally closing my folder and placing the pad along with what he had just written on it back in his front pocket.

"And..." I struggled to form the words. "I'll be okay...not in here?"

Doctor Howard smiled. It was warm and inviting, the type you had to practice multiple times to get just right. "Are you afraid of hurting someone or yourself?"

I shook my head.

"I didn't think so." He stood and shook my hand as I remained sitting. "I know this is scary, but we're here to help you. There are so many patients here that our staff is worn thin and I'd rather release those who would not benefit from being locked up within four walls. I'm of the opinion that the longer a more or less healthy person stays here, the worse their mental state becomes, no?"

I nodded. After my first few days, I had already seen more than one person who would most likely be locked away the rest of their lives. I wondered if they were once like me. If maybe they had been released they would have been okay.

"Sound good, Corbin?"

I stood too. He slid my sketchbook back to me and I took it in my arms and hugged it to my chest. "Yes," I said. "Thank you."

CHAPTER
FIFTEEN

MOST OF MY STAY AT Cedar Ridge was uneventful. I woke up, went to all my activities, talked to people only long enough to show those looking on that I was being sociable. I ate my spongy eggs and cold spaghetti. I spoke up in group and shared my feelings. Everyone in charge thought I was a cooperative, well behaved, and normal patient. I never talked about Six. We talked enough at night. That was our time and I didn't want to bring him up under the harsh florescent lights, while the sun shone in through the windows, when I was fully awake and fully aware of just how crazy it all sounded.

I went to bed early most nights, just as people started winding down after evening meds. I understood why my roommate was asleep and awake before everyone else: it was awful to watch people of all ages—eighteen to fifty—powering down like battery-powered action figures in a neglectful child's toy box. I would lie down under my uncomfortable blanket, waiting for my sleeping pill to create its familiar buzz in my head and make my limbs light. I would usually get a few hours before I was awake again, the voice whispering in my ear as if nothing had changed. And really, nothing had.

Wake up, it said. It was strange, the direct command. Usually, I was just awake. I never had to be told. When I rolled over, intent on ignoring it like I always did at first, the blankets fell off, leaving me cold.

I tried to grasp onto the fabric, but it slipped from my fingers like a silky snake that had just shed its skin. I knew it was purposeful, but I didn't know whose idea it was. "Why?" I whispered into the dark.

You need to get up, said the voice. *You need to do something for me.*

I couldn't open my eyes, but I tried to so badly. "Let me see first."

Stand first, the voice countered.

Taking a deep breath, I stood almost angrily in the center of the room. I leaned my hands on the bookshelf in front of me, my legs cold in the air conditioned room.

My roommate tossed her body to the opposite side; I hoped she was facing the wall. "They'll be doing checks soon," I whispered.

I know, said the voice. *I only need you for a moment.*

I wanted to ask what he was going to do, what he thought he was going to accomplish by making it seem like I was crazier than I had been when I first checked into this looney bin. But I was more afraid of the deadly quiet and how I was disturbing it.

Every bare footstep, every whisper, every movement of a limb. It all created something that wasn't there before and it scared me.

Ask to go to the bathroom, said the voice.

I wanted to ask why, but I didn't have to.

I need to be near water, said the voice simply, like it was an obvious notion I should have thought of myself. *Just turn on the sink for me.*

Sudden anger flared in my chest, hot and causing my blood to pump faster, bringing the beating to my ears. "Why don't you just go walking again?" I spat into the dark, my eyes completely closed.

A pause came then, which usually meant the voice was either thinking or receding back to the recesses of my mind. *I am weak,* it said right near my face. I imagined the shadow of it looming over me, wavering like a quivering voice.

I crossed my arms. "I want something in return."

Of course, it said quickly, with a hint of amusement.

"No more making me look or feel crazy," I whispered as strongly as I could without raising my voice. "Leave me alone. At least when people are around. Please."

I felt my vocal cords tighten, my voice cut off. I was crying by myself in the dark, pleading with myself to leave me alone. Maybe I did belong here.

Don't cry, my love, the voice cooed. I felt a light touch against my cheek, as if someone had wiped the tears away. *I only need you to take me to the bathroom,* it repeated. *I promise, I will help you get out of here.*

"You'll leave me alone," I corrected through a quiet sob.

Yesssss, it hissed gently. *Just stop crying. It...hurts me.*

I sniffed, wrapping my hands around myself even tighter, like I could hold every loose piece together this way. My eyes had adjusted to the dark, and it was no surprise I saw nothing but the bare room, the dim nightlight, the bright strip of florescence from the nurses' station that leaked under the heavy curtain.

Slowly, I touched the fabric separating our room from the rest of the ward. I clenched my fingers around it, letting the full weight of the rough material seep its way into my skin. I couldn't remember the last time something felt so heavy, so dense in the dark.

As soon as the smooth sound of the curtain sliding on the metal rod registered to my ears, a nurse was in front of me. She was a middle aged woman whose pink cartoon scrubs were too big. She had the stance of someone who had been interrupted during the night by many an unpleasant thing, given the expression on her face.

"Do you need something..." she glanced at the wipe board just to the left of the door, probably not thinking I could see the movement, "Corbin?"

"I..." I had to clear my throat. "I need to use the bathroom."

The nurse checked her watch like she was waiting for a cake to be done baking. "It's only been two hours since lights out," she said with a finality that meant she didn't believe I had to actually use the bathroom.

It was true, I didn't. But if it actually helped trick my mind, or my fake mind, or whatever the hell it was into leaving me alone, I had to be convincing.

"I think it's the new medicine I'm on," I said quickly. "It gives me dry mouth so I have to drink a lot more water than I'm used to." I said this conversationally, like we were on the same level without losing any of the respect the nurse deserved. She held all the keys to this labyrinth; I couldn't afford to get on her bad side.

The nurse sighed. "Alright," she said, checking her watch again as if the cake timer were about to go off at any second. "I have checks in five minutes," she said. "You think you can be back in bed by then?"

I smiled, feigning gratefulness. "Yes," I said dramatically. "Thank you so much!"

The nurse actually cracked a smile. "I'll start at the other end of the hall," she said, giving me a small wink like we were already sharing a secret that no one knew about.

"Thank you so much," I repeated.

With that, I turned on my heel and walked quickly in the direction of the bathroom.

I was grateful she had opted not to follow me. I may have earned enough points or I may have distracted her from her routine; I didn't care. There was a clock on the wall above a small desk outside of the bathroom. I signed my name and recorded the time—10:00—then stepped into the bathroom.

I was alone, thank God. "Okay," I said to myself. At least that was who I told myself I was saying it to. My shaking hands reached for the faucet and turned on both taps full blast. "Do what you need to do."

I realized that the voice had not spoken in quite some time, but I figured it would come back at any moment.

Impatiently tapping my foot on the cold linoleum, I sighed, feeling utterly stupid and even more insane than I originally gave myself credit for. Shaking my head, I reached for the taps again.

Don't, whispered the voice.

I sighed again, watching as the water went directly down the drain, the white noise of it filling the empty space. "Hurry up," I whispered.

Go into a stall, said the voice somewhere from behind me. *I do not want you to see.*

I thought about planting my feet firmly where I stood, telling who or whatever it was that was talking to me that no, I wasn't going to go anywhere. If this was something that came from my mind, I should be able to deal with what it actually looked like, regardless of what it said.

But outside, the clock was ticking and the night nurse was making her way slowly down the hall, opening curtains and counting sleeping, troubled minds. I couldn't afford to argue.

Without a word, I stepped into the first stall and closed the door, latching it behind me.

There was nothing after that. Just the sound of water rushing, liquid against porcelain.

Then there was the sound of something else, something new. It wasn't so different from the sound of water that it made me question it right away. It was more like someone disrupting the flow, like someone was washing their hands.

Without thinking about it, I peeked through the gap in the stall, expecting what I always found when I heard something strange and looked to see what it was: nothing.

But it wasn't nothing.

CHAPTER
SIXTEEN

THERE IS A TIME IN everyone's life where they question what it's all about. What makes them *them* and what makes others not them. Sometimes they question if there is a God if they were brought up to believe in one. Sometimes they question if there is something before or after they became conscious to this existence. If they were an insect before a human embryo. If they will become some great wash of light in the sky once they've stopped breathing.

This was like that.

I took one look outside of the bathroom stall and questioned everything that had brought me to this point. I had tried so desperately to stay on a clean path, one that only led to a bright future and happiness for me and my mother, but I couldn't help but think that somewhere I had been led astray. Had some big bad wolf convinced me to pick flowers? Had birds eaten my breadcrumbs? Was I forever doomed to walk in the dark, dense woods because of one mistake that was so small I could not even remember what it was now?

A small smudge of a shadow was streaked above the mirrorless sink. A stain from fingers, but not from a human. They were more like claw marks, something that I had never seen in my life before. I thought it couldn't get worse than that print above the sink, but when I looked to the water itself, it had turned a deep brown, as if all the sewage under the tiles had been brought up to the surface through the pipes.

I inhaled sharply, as if the air around me had turned into something thick and I was being forced to get my oxygen through a thin, cracked straw.

The image shifted from liquid to solid in a matter of seconds. What was once a coffee stain was now broad shoulders. What had been something amorphous now had legs to stand on, a head.

Those were the only features: a shadow in the bright lights of the bathroom; the smell of dead leaves in the otherwise sterile, alcoholic environment.

It did not shift, did not move. It merely stood there, water running in the silence as I tried to remain calm, watching it as much as anticipating it to go away.

I thought I told you to close your eyes.

The voice wasn't a whisper now. Like the stain into the shadow, it had formed into something more solid, yet still decidedly not completely there. If I swept my hand across it, the image, the voice—all of it would distort.

I snapped my eyes tightly shut.

"Will you hurry up?" I whispered, unable to raise my voice. My head was spinning and my chest ached. I wondered if I should pull the emergency handle in the stall so a nurse would come rushing in and give me something to sink my mind into something more pleasant. I could go somewhere my life wasn't complicated and only rely on the most basic of human functions, no thought required.

But I decided against it. *It'll be gone*, I reminded myself as I sat down on the cold toilet seat. All I had to do was survive this one moment in time, get back to my room, and it would leave me alone so I could leave this place. All I had to do was make it through the next few silent moments with the water running in the empty lavatory, the smell of leaves in my head, and the shadow at the sink. Just a few feet away from the barrier of blush pink bathroom stall door I was hiding behind.

Nearly done, the voice said. It was even fuller this time, almost completely there. An image of something more solid came to me behind my closed eyelids, a man with broad shoulders and the face of the man I had drawn what seemed like lifetimes ago. I gripped the handicap railing to my left so I wouldn't fall over.

Then, as if I asked it to out loud, the water turned off, a drip the only indication that it was ever on. It resounded off the tiled walls. I waited to open my eyes, my hand still clenched around the rail for support. I wondered if whatever had to be done was finished; if it was safe to exit and crawl under the covers as my roommate tossed and turned. I was determined to let sleep suck me down into a deep dark hole, determined to forget everything I had just seen.

No voice came, just the intermittent drip, the footsteps of the nurse down the hall, closing in on my room no doubt. Slowly, I opened my eyes. It seemed to take a lot of effort to peek through my lashes, through the crack in the stall into the rest of the bathroom. Nothing there. No smudges, no stains, no sludge, no shadow hunched over the sink.

Shaking hands reached the cold metal latch and slid it with a loud, hollow sound that could only come in the middle of the night when everyone was asleep and things that no one else had seen were happening. My slippers scuffed against the linoleum and I held onto the wall as I left the bathroom; I stared at the faucet the entire time until I was once again out in the hall.

I could see half of the nurse's body peeking out from one of the rooms, just two down from mine. She made her way back to room number seventeen, the wipe board with mine and my roommate's name written outside. I slipped into my rumpled bed, the itchy fabric sending goose bumps shooting down my arms and legs. My heart pounded in my temples, making it impossible to concentrate on anything else. Sinking my head into the pillow, I tried to relax the muscles in my neck, the tension in my spine, but no relief came. I was perpetually ready to bolt, should the image of the shadow ever come back, now that I was in the dark.

A flashlight shone into the dark room; the nurse was checking in on us, counting sleeping heads and making sure no one was crying, reading, throwing up, or cutting themselves with a spork they had stolen at lunchtime.

"Greene."

Hearing my last name in the middle of the night was somehow more terrifying than seeing the disembodied voice suddenly embodied in the light of the bathroom. I sat bolt upright in bed, my dark hair whipping me in the face and the harsh flashlight blinding me.

The nurse stood there, not bothering to shy away the light. "Forgetting something?" she said in a tone that wasn't quite scolding, but it wasn't pleasant either. It simply held the tone of someone who worked too much and put up with too much shit for not enough pay.

"Huh?" I asked groggily. At least I hoped that's how I sounded. Not scared. Not troubled. If I sounded like that, the nurse would report it to the doctor, then the doctor would want to talk about it. Even if they somehow didn't manage to pull the truth from me, I would most likely walk away with a shiny new batch of pills and maybe even another week's stay to see how I adjusted to them.

She sighed heavily. My roommate turned in closer to the wall, still fast asleep. She could sleep through anything. I wished I was that lucky.

The nurse handed me the clipboard from outside of the bathroom, the pen slinging back and forth on its twine cord. "You didn't sign out," she said. "It's 10:20."

"Oh," I said, relieved. "Sorry."

She smiled sympathetically. "Yeah, meds make you forget things too," she said. "Just don't let it happen again. I don't have time to chase down everyone who forgets something in this place." She snorted under her breath, like she was thinking of something that used to be a joke but now it just made her sad. "God knows there isn't enough time in the day."

I wrote down the time and signed my name quickly, handing the nurse back the clipboard. Finally, the light was removed from my face and I could see the dim room once more, save for a few colorful spots around my vision.

"Now go to sleep," she said. "Try not to have to pee until morning. They see you signing in and out at all hours and they'll want to talk about it." She said this like she was offering some sage advice, as if she had been through this very thing herself.

"Thanks," I said.

The nurse nodded once and shut the curtain, leaving it open a crack. A small amount of light filtered in, and I was afraid it would cast more shadows and cause me more confusion.

Closing my eyes tightly, I lay on my back and brought the uncomfortable blanket up to my chin. I stared at the clock on the wall until it read three. I knew it was only a matter of time before I smelled the dead leaves, felt the mattress dip in on one side, and the hair moved from my face.

But the time came and went without a sound.

CHAPTER
SEVENTEEN

DOCTOR HOWARD SAT ACROSS FROM me in his usual spot, behind the long, fake wooden table that was far too large for the room, in one of the plastic chairs. Today his was blue; mine was orange. He opened my manila folder and uncapped a pen, which although it wasn't one he had stolen from a bank, I could see faint teeth marks near the top. "So," he said. "How are you?"

"Good," I said, crossing my legs and folding my fingers together on top of my knee. It wasn't a lie, but it wasn't exactly the truth. The voice had not returned for the week I was on the medicine and I didn't know if it was the drugs or if the night in the bathroom made any difference. Maybe it was all connected. I would ask Doctor Howard if I knew for a fact that it wouldn't earn me another two weeks.

"Adjusting to the meds well?" he asked without looking up, marking something on a clean sheet of yellow paper. I couldn't read the small print. "No more hallucinations?"

"Yeah," I said simply.

Doctor Howard raised an eyebrow, glancing over at me before returning his gaze to the chart in front of him.

"I mean," I decided to backtrack slightly. I didn't want to sound *too* perfectly fine. That would only make him suspicious. "I get dry mouth and sometimes I'm really tired, but other than that, it's not too bad."

He seemed more satisfied with this answer and smiled slightly.

"And I haven't seen or heard anything since I started taking it." That wasn't a lie at all, save for the one last farewell.

Doctor Howard smiled even more broadly then, pleased that his initial diagnosis and treatment had not been contested in any way. "That's great, Corbin," he said, jotting down a few more notes. "How does it feel?" he asked.

I didn't like the way he asked the question. He was proud that Six was gone and I...well, I wasn't. I was only happy that I was one step closer to getting out of this hellhole I had forced myself into. "Well," I said, suddenly at a loss for words. "I don't know. Kind of...weird."

He jotted something else down. "Weird?" he asked, folding his hands on top of his notes. His tone was light, easy, like my answer couldn't send the walls around us crashing down.

"Well...a little."

He looked pointedly at me through his thick rimmed glasses. "Try to explain."

I took a deep breath and stared at my hands. "I guess I'm just used to having this voice...expecting it around the corner, you know?"

"Do you miss it?" he asked seriously, but somehow keeping judgment from his voice.

"No," I said, and I knew that it was a lie as it left my mouth.

"It's okay if you do," said Doctor Howard. "This entity was something that kept you busy, something that followed you for a lot of your time. It's only natural to feel strange now that you're without it."

"It is?" I asked.

He nodded. "Absolutely. So long as you stay healthy and gain distance from this voice, you'll be just fine."

Now he shut my file, leaned down, and took something from his briefcase on the floor. I watched with wide eyes as he opened another folder and took out a packet of clean white paper. Packets like that looked important. Packets like that meant business.

Doctor Howard wrote something with the blue, chewed ballpoint pen for a long time. He scribbled and scribbled and then flipped a page, checking things off and writing here and there. "So," he said after the longest heartbeat of my life. "I'm releasing you as of today, under the condition that you talk to a therapist once a week."

I couldn't believe the words tumbling out of his mouth, as they ricocheted against the large table and scattered to the floor around my uncomfortable chair like Scrabble tiles. "Really?" I asked, my throat tight as if I was about to cry. I wouldn't, though. Not now. Not when I was so close.

"Really." Doctor Howard smiled, looking me straight in the eyes. "I told you," he said. "You don't belong here."

He handed over the paperwork and instructed me to hand it to the nurses' desk. They would take it from there. He congratulated me on my release and made me promise he wouldn't see me back there again.

Walking to the nurses' desk with the heavy weight of the paperwork in my hands was strange. It was like one of those dreams where you're running down a hallway trying to escape some boogey man or monster, but the door or light or whatever it is at the end keeps moving away. You fear you'll never reach it; you fear that whatever is chasing you will catch up.

"Everything alright?" asked a nurse I didn't recognize. She was tall with the most beautiful dark chocolate skin I had ever seen. I made a mental note to try to draw her later, if I could remember what she looked like. I would make her an angel or a saint. Maybe paint clouds behind her as a great beacon of light shone on her face, making her deep brown eyes glitter.

"Oh," she said as she glanced at the paper in my hands. It was suddenly heavier than it had been on the long walk from the office to the desk. I handed over the stack of stapled pages and the woman took it with her perfectly manicured hand. I took great note of this. Hands were important. They always said so much.

The nurse scanned the front page, where Doctor Howard had spent the most time scribbling. Then she turned a few pages, looking them over as well, only not as long before flipping through the rest of the document. "Well," she said with a smile as she finished reading the last page. She took a pen from the desk and handed it to me. "All you need to do is sign here and we'll get you all set to leave."

I took the pen between my fingers and dropped it on the floor. It clacked against the linoleum and I picked it up, this time with a tighter grip. I signed the dotted line and dated it. It had been exactly two weeks since I had checked in.

I stared at the line for a few seconds after signing. I couldn't seem to take my eyes off of it, feeling like I had cheated or had *been* cheated in some way. I couldn't exactly figure out which.

"Alright," said the nurse, taking the pen gently from me and the packet slipped from my hands as she placed them both on the desk. "If you'll follow me, I need to supervise you as you gather your belongings."

I let the nurse get a head start. I watched as she sashayed down the hall like she was almost comfortable there, in her bright pink scrubs. I followed at a close distance, not wanting anyone looking to think I felt the same way. There was loyalty in these walls, and if I ever somehow found myself back here by some horrible fortune, I wasn't going to make any enemies by rubbing my release in anyone's face. They would be jealous enough that I was leaving I didn't need anything else to make them angry or make them think I was one of them and not with the group because I was deemed healthier than the rest of them. Maybe I was just luckier.

We made it to my room in less time than it seemed to walk to the desk, and the nurse stood at the door and watched as I dragged the suitcase my mother had dropped off so long ago from under the bed and started hastily packing the few belongings I had. I even put on my leather jacket, deciding that the heat wasn't all that important outside. If I was leaving this place, I was leaving as myself, not the person who had lived within these walls for two weeks without shaving, without wearing anything besides a glorified hospital gown, pajama pants, and stiff slippers with the bottoms that never seemed clean.

"Is that all?" the nurse asked once the suitcase was zippered and in hand.

I searched the room for any last remnants, not wanting to leave any evidence of my presence. I found my sketchpad sticking out on the overstuffed bookshelf. I grasped the heavy volume and yanked until it came off and was no longer a part of this place, but back in my arms where it belonged. I didn't think about all of the drawings inside of it.

"That's all," I said almost easily as I popped up the handle of my suitcase and began to roll it out of the room.

"Everyone's at breakfast right now," said the nurse as we made our way back to the main lobby, to the front doors. "You want to wait so you can say goodbye?"

I shook my head. "I don't really know anyone that well anyway."

She nodded knowingly. "You're a short-timer," she said. "Nothing to be ashamed of."

Smiling, she placed a hand on the small of my back and we walked the rest of the way to the lobby together, the wheels of my suitcase against the linoleum the only sound besides our footsteps.

CHAPTER
EIGHTEEN

AS SOON AS I GOT home, I got rid of anything that reminded me of Six. I tore out the sketches of the winged creature and the man's face. I gathered the feathers I was given the morning after my black out as well as the few I kept for myself before I went away. I stuffed them into the garbage outside and made sure they were well covered with trash and goop before going back in the house. When I got to my room again, I sat on the pink satin comforter and stared at the bookshelf where the box sat. The dark wood looked like chocolate to me, the intricate metalwork around the edges its silver wrapper. I wanted nothing more than to reach out and hold it to my chest, absorb its sweetness and never let go. I didn't know why or how, but this box was connected to everything. I couldn't fall back into old habits if I wanted to leave it behind me.

It took what seemed like a long time for me to finally stand; it was like I didn't trust my own legs to carry me all the way, my own hands to let go when I told them to.

I decided that rather than throw the box away, I would hide it. I thought about putting it somewhere in the living room or kitchen, amongst stacks of antique china we never ate off of or between books on a long forgotten shelf. But Mom kept inventory better than a warehouse worker. Although she had a ton of odds and ends that many people had discarded at various stages of their lives, she knew each one intimately. Every painted flower, every chip in porcelain. She would no doubt notice that my present was a new addition, and I didn't want her to think I didn't like it. She was worried about me—and her ability as a mother—enough.

Besides, when I thought about the box in the same place as the drawings and feathers, my chest became tight and my vision blurred. Those other things were more or less replaceable. Not this. It physically hurt to have something that was so beautiful dumped like it was trash.

In the end, the place I chose wasn't far from where it sat in the first place. Directly in front of my bed, to the left of the nightlight, was my closet. Inside that, I had storage containers filled with old sketchpads and things like Christmas decorations that Mom couldn't jam into the attic. It was in a giant, musty grey one, under Halloween costumes that hadn't fit me since the first grade, where I hid the box. I watched as the heavy wood sank into the pillow of cheap crushed purple velvet of some disco-lady costume and the lid shut with a slight jingle as a jester's hat at the bottom moved. When I pushed the storage container aside, hiding it between hanging sweaters and dresses, it still hurt knowing I wouldn't roll over in the middle of the night to see it there, staring back at me from the shelf. But this was what I had to do in order to feel better. The last thing I needed was the voice coming back because I was feeding into my delusions.

What I *wanted*, however, was entirely different.

The first night with the box in its new home was quiet. It was also my first night home in my own bed, without someone checking in on me every few hours (if I didn't count Mom), so maybe that was why it was so silent. I turned on my iPod just to give my mind something to concentrate on, but it seemed too loud, the headphones too constricting. Turning it off and rolling over, I waited hours for my even newer sleeping pills to kick in and whisk me off to a dreamless sleep.

I tried telling myself that I was just restless after a long journey. Over the last couple of weeks, I had gotten used to the squeaking of shoes, the jingling of the bathroom keys, and the distant sounds of troubled minds as they tried to fight the monsters in their nightmares. I told myself that I shouldn't count the voice among those comforting sounds.

But I couldn't ignore the pull—deep in my chest and the back of my head. It was like being sucked up in a tide that I couldn't control, pulling and pushing me toward the crack under my closet door. I imagined climbing out of bed, rushing over to the closet, throwing open the door and going back to that cold, grey storage container and liberating the box from its cheap fabric prison. I would sit on the floor in my closet with the lights off and the door closed. I wanted to fill the box with loose change I had lying around. I wanted to go for a walk along the beach and find stones and shells to put inside. I wanted to polish the wood and shine the metal, apologize for ever sticking it in such a horrible place, and make it a new one, right next to my bed on its own pillow so I could turn around at any point during the night and see it. So it could see *me*.

There had been no voice since the night in the bathroom, but I was afraid of what it meant to be so attached to an inanimate object that I couldn't even see from my bed. Maybe I had only traded in one problem for another.

JORDAN CAME TO SEE ME about a week after I came back. We didn't talk about what happened before I left or where I went, but I apologized again and vaguely explained that I was "going through some shit" and she seemed to understand well enough. I could tell that behind her eyes, when I said I was sorry, she was ticking something off. Some list of reasons she should or should not trust me. I would have to be careful around her and not betray her ever again. I knew that much. I didn't need to lose my only friend—especially because of something imaginary.

We spent most out my time drawing, posing, and painting. Most things were abstract. Inkblots that I was sure that if I ever had to go back to Cedar Ridge could keep Doctor Howard entertained for hours. Jodan kept a steady pace on one painting of me holding an umbrella as tiny hot air balloons floated around me. She was working on getting the details of my face just right. According to her, if the face was botched, you might as well scrap the whole piece. No use wasting time on an entire painting if you were only going to scrap it.

I didn't really disagree with her, but after the face in my notebook, I decided to stay away from human subject matter for the time being. If Jordan thought it was strange that I had switched from hyper detail to amorphous blobs, she didn't say anything. By the end of the day, I had four canvases drying around my room, all of which meant nothing to me.

I was unable to pinpoint what my problem was. If I was just out of practice, afraid, or out of ideas.

"Don't worry about it," Jordan said as she clapped me on the back. "You know how Picasso had all those phases? Blue and brown and boring?"

I snorted. "I don't think I've learned about the boring phase."

She adjusted the strap of her portfolio on her shoulder as she studied one of my canvases. This one was still a blob, but sharper around the edges versus round. There were more lines and angles to this one. "The point is," she said, blowing her bangs out of her face with a puff of breath, "you're going through a phase. You've got to get all the shit out before you can paint something good."

I brightened slightly at her words. "You think so?"

She shrugged. "Happens to me a few times a year."

We made plans to meet up again sometime over the week to do it again. I hoped my "phase" would be over by then.

When I followed Jordan out, Mom was in the kitchen making dinner. I had been home only a few weeks, and in that time she had decided that it was better that we eat at the table like a family—other families did it, so we should too.

The table was cleared off, its contents on the counter or the floor now. Mom started out by digging out some random cookbook most likely from the sixties and making gross shit like beef wellington and chicken a la king. Now she stuck to easy things, like spaghetti and meatballs, mac n' cheese, basically anything that required little more than boiling water and adding the appropriate sauce.

She even lit a candle in the middle of the table and dimmed the lights. I think it was meant to make it feel more like an intimate thing, but I felt like we were two spinsters trying to conduct a séance.

"Did you have a good day today, sweetie?" she asked from across her wineglass of water. Mom didn't drink; it messed with her meds.

I watched the candle light flicker against her skin as she smiled tightly. We didn't talk about my time away either. Mom had only come once while I was to Cedar Ridge to drop off some of my clothes. I tried not to think about how defeated she looked standing there with my battered suitcase, wearing stained sweatpants and a shirt that was too big for her. When I looked into her deep brown eyes that day, it was like I was seeing the depths of the abyss that awaited me—and this was only the beginning. I had much further to fall before I reached the bottom.

It was like that whenever I looked at her. No matter how hard she smiled, no matter how diligently we avoided the subject, it was like the eyes of a fish stared back at me. They looked but didn't really see. Maybe she didn't want to.

"Fine," I said. "It felt good to paint again."

Mom spooned some of her food into her mouth. Even she looked like she didn't want to eat it. I didn't bother chewing. I just let whatever it was slip down my throat, thankful I couldn't really see what it was in the dim light. "That's great, honey," she said. "I'm glad you're home."

I smiled slightly just to put her at ease. "Me too, Mom."

We ate the rest of our meal in silence, the way we did most things lately. When I couldn't stomach, I emptied my plate and washed it in the sink, setting it on the rack to dry. Mom followed suit just as I turned around to leave and retreat back to my room, causing the candle to flicker and the light to dance along the wall connecting the kitchen and living room.

I could have sworn I saw something behind her, but it turned out to just be her shadow. Passing by Mom and switching places with her—me at the table and her at the sink—I blew out the candle and turned on the overhead light before heading back into my room.

I took my sleeping pill early. It was only nine, but there wasn't much else that I wanted to do, so while I waited for it to take effect, I cleaned up some of my paint and scrap paper.

I couldn't help but keep looking over at the blobs I had spent the better part of my day painting. None of them had any distinct shapes, and I couldn't remember setting out to make anything modern or abstract. I just knew that I wanted to feel my hand wrapped around a brush, the thick paint in its bristles as it glided over the stretched fabric of the canvas. Maybe it didn't matter what I painted. Maybe Jordan was right: I just had to get some shit out.

As I moved across my room, I capped paint here and gathered dirty paper towels there. I kept my eyes trained on my tasks, not wanting to so much as glance at the closet where my beloved box now rested.

Once all the paint and paper was away and my room was more or less back to its adolescent-looking state, I piled the now dry canvases against the bottom of my bookcase, facing away from me so they didn't watch me as I slept. It was strange. While I was painting them, I liked the slick blackness of the shapes, the control—or lack thereof—that came with it. One color that represented them all against the white background. The thought somehow soothed me. But now that the moment of creating them had passed, I was almost leery of them. I didn't know what they meant.

The memory of the voice echoed in my mind: *I am all. I am none. I am the earth. The fire and the flood. The sun and the rain. The mouse and the crow.*

As I laid my head against the pillow, I reached my hand underneath, smoothing the soft material my fingertips came into contact with. I let myself sink into the mattress, the sheets, the pillowcase. I let the world around me buzz in the soft glow of the pills in my system as my eyes became heavy and I grasped the only feather I hadn't thrown away in my hand.

CHAPTER
NINETEEN

THE REST OF THE MONTH was one hundred percent voice-free. After a while, I almost didn't notice its absence. I almost didn't miss it.

It was easier to ignore with my nights taken up by new, different sounds.

At first, I thought nothing of them. One night as I lay awake waiting for the pills to take over, a soft pinging began outside my window. It was like someone was throwing stones against the glass or water droplets left over from a heavy storm trickled down the drainage pipe. I thought nothing of them. Maybe that was the problem. If I paid attention the first time, maybe they wouldn't have grown into something else.

They became louder. The sound of a screen door slamming over and over again when there was no possible way anyone was awake and repeating the movement. Knocking, loud and clear from inside the walls surrounding me, like someone was trapped and asking to be let in or out.

After the living better part of the August hearing these things, I realized that they only happened when I was near or in my room. I never heard them in the kitchen or living area, when I was at work or in my car. I contemplated maybe trying to sleep somewhere else on some of my more desperate nights, pillow over my head and sweating.

But that was ridiculous. I wasn't going to be chased out of my room by my own mind.

I had started seeing Doctor Howard as an outpatient once a week and then once every other week, per his instructions. We talked about trivial things mostly, but he determined these things were enough to tell him I was getting better. I wanted to mention these new sounds to him, but every time I tried to open my mouth, something stopped me.

Maybe it was time he upped my meds.

It was after a particularly noisy night that I shuffled into the kitchen one afternoon and sat down with a box of Frosted Flakes as Mom scraped the burnt bits off her toast with a crooked spoon, crumbs falling on the paper plate in front of her. "Good morning, sweetie," she said without looking up. Mom was wearing her robe again and her hair was dirty, like she hadn't washed it in a few days.

"Morning," I mumbled as I smelled a carton of milk I wasn't sure how long had sat in the fridge. It seemed fine, but you never knew in this house.

The table was once again cluttered. Mom's new hobby was

clipping coupons she would most likely never get around to using, so every spare surface was draped in newspapers and circular ads. She had stopped insisting we sit and eat dinner together every night. It was easier to leave things as they were.

I hunched over the counter and poured my milk onto the stale flakes, my jaw popping as I chewed. I had begun grinding my teeth in my sleep, maybe to drown out all the other sounds.

There was a new wind chime hanging in the window above the sink. This one was made out of some kind of thinly sliced, polished rocks. They were purple and glinted in the early afternoon light.

"That's cool," I commented.

Mom looked up from her spread out papers, swallowed her dry toast and said, "It was grandma's. I found it the other day."

My mother's mother was notorious for her strangeness. Maybe even more so than my mom. But it was different. When old people were weird it was endearing, maybe even sad once in a while. It wasn't like us.

"Oh yeah?" I asked, wiping a stray droplet of milk off the counter with my finger.

I loved my grandma. She was a tiny woman with a loud voice and didn't take crap from anyone. She lived in a retirement community in a tiny trailer that she had painted bright yellow and there were always these colorful fake flowers hanging around. Mom used to tell me stories of when she was little. How grandma was the bravest woman she knew because they lived near a graveyard and she was the only one who wasn't afraid to walk by it at night. She told me once, over tea and stale cookies as she watched me while Mom was out, that the dead weren't so bad. It was the living that we had to be afraid of. The dead were just looking for some company. Grandma believed she could communicate with these lost souls as easily as she could pick up a phone. She complained about it sometimes, how she was only one person and she didn't have time to entertain the ghosts' ideas of her helping them make a sandwich or avenge their deaths.

When I was older, Mom would tell me it was the schizophrenia that made her believe this, and it was like someone telling me that Santa wasn't real.

Mom smiled as she continued her work. "It was just buried underneath a bunch of junk."

Everything was. One day we would both wake up and find ourselves buried too.

I spooned more soggy Frosted Flakes onto my spoon and let it hover in front of me for a few seconds. I stared at the surface of the little flattened pieces of corn, some glistening with slightly off milk, some completely unrecognizable.

A black spider crawled out from under one of them and I dropped my spoon back in the bowl, the sudden clang of metal on ceramic loud in the quiet and sunny room.

"Everything okay?" Mom asked as she turned to me, not completely alarmed but not uninterested.

After a second to catch my breath, I grasped the handle of the spoon and filtered through the milk, lifting soggy sections of cereal the thing could be hiding under. I couldn't find it.

"Corbin?" Mom asked when I didn't answer.

No longer hungry, I dumped the entire bowl into the sink and slowly and carefully rinsed everything down the drain before turning on the garbage disposal. It wasn't there. "Fine," I finally answered.

Retreating back to my room, I tried to convince myself that it was nothing as I changed into a t-shirt and jeans. I kept seeing the spider sitting amongst my cereal, nestled in between two flakes and safe from the river of white liquid until I lifted it in my spoon and exposed its hiding place. Maybe in the time it took me to drop my spoon and pick it back up again, the thing had somehow skittered to the floor or somewhere else on the counter. Maybe I had drowned it and it was nothing more than a ball of black legs and body resembling a milk bubble and that's why I didn't see it when I poured the bowl's contents down the drain. Or the worst theory: it could have been my imagination.

Deciding that thinking like this would only drive me more insane, I shrugged it off and set up my easel and supplies to get ready to figure out how I could turn my unfortunate blobs into something remotely recognizable.

I dragged the stack of canvases from where they leaned against my bookcase and set up all three of them on their own easels. I had positioned them each so I could sit on my bed and take in all of them at once. It would be good to compare them side by side to try and figure out what my "vision" or whatever was. The one on the right was basically a black canvas at this point, only slight scratches and slivers of white showing through.

The middle one was the sharp edged blob, and the third was supposed to be an ink splatter-like image, but up close, it looked like someone had spilled really strong coffee on it. I had run out of black paint and had to use a lot of water to make it stretch.

Setting my old wooden palate and cup of water on my desk nearby, I took out a large brush and uncapped a new tube of black paint. All I wanted was black. When I looked at the greens, reds, yellows and blues of my paint box, the colors made my eyes hurt and stomach turn. Loading as much black paint as I could onto the brush without it dripping onto the carpet beneath my bare feet, I moved closer to the coffee-stained canvas. For whatever reason, I couldn't stop staring at it. The swirls of diluted inkiness were thin in the places the water settled and thicker where it had dried before it became too saturated. For the life of me, I could not remember setting out to paint such a thing. I could not remember adding so much water to the paint that it turned brown. Although I didn't necessarily set out to paint any of these pieces, this was the only one that made me uneasy. The only one I felt a strange pull toward, much like the one I tried to ignore that was coming from my closet. I wanted it to look like the other two canvases. I wanted to cover up whatever it was. Touching brush to canvas, the smell began immediately.

It wasn't the usual acrylic-plastic smell that came naturally with the cheap paint I used. It was like a swamp had driven by my open window. Something dark and murky; I couldn't tell what was underneath. Then the scent changed. Sharp and crisp in my nostrils, it stopped my brush mid-stroke and I had to place it on the desk to keep from dropping it and making a mess. Before I could turn back to the painting, the tapping started. Slight, soft and fast, there was something on my window, then something on the wall. Of course, when I looked, there was nothing. And it only grew louder. Knocks. Bangs.

The smell of fire and burning leaves surrounded me next. I was afraid to look anywhere—around me showed nothing and the painting showed me too much of what I didn't understand. I sat on the ground between my three easels, clamping my hands over my ears and squeezing my eyes shut so tight that they watered.

The muffled knocks droned on. There was no rhythm, no reason, no pattern I could discern. The smell of smoke became stronger in my nostrils. So strong and heavy that it burned the back of my throat and I had to open my eyes.

A small spiral of grey emanated from the center of the canvas. Before I could comprehend that what I was seeing was real, the entire middle of the painting burst into flames, the center turning into black ash and falling to the carpet below. Without thinking, I grabbed my dirty paint water and threw it at the canvas, extinguishing the flames in one fluid motion.

When things slowed down once again, I realized that the sounds and smells had stopped. Now all that remained was the pounding of my pulse as blood rushed to my head. It took me what seemed like a very long time to bring myself closer to the painting—or what was left of it. I blinked a few times, convinced that my mind had just made this up. Things didn't just burst into flames for no reason. But it was there, plain as black and white.

A hole that was the size of a half dollar stared back at me, the edges stiff yet fragile. I reached out with shaking fingers to touch the area surrounding part of the hole that still glowed orange with dying embers and it was warm. When I blew on the fabric, it turned bright yellow, as if I would bring it back to life, but I stopped breathing onto it and it faded back to grey.

Straight through the hole was the door to my closet, and as soon as my eyes locked onto it, one loud, resounding knock filled my ears.

Anger flared deep within my belly. So was this how it was going to be? I clenched my fists at my sides. I was going to see these things and hear these things from now on no matter what? What if I just ignored the obvious call directed at me? What if I chose to still believe this was all in my head and I could go back to the doctor at any time to adjust my medication and make it all go away?

Would I always be wondering what awaited me on any given day, that when I was least expecting it, things like this would creep up on me and ruin any sense of normalcy I had?

I let the anger take over. This wasn't fair. This wasn't what I wanted. This wasn't how my life was supposed to be. People like my mother and grandmother lived this way. Not me. I was different.

I flipped the canvas onto the floor, tearing through the easel as I stomped toward the closet. I swung open the door and dove into the rack of clothing covering the storage container.

"Is this what you want?" I whispered as I tore the lid off,

scraping my knuckles on the hard plastic and not even caring. "For me to be crazy? For me to let you out and ruin my life?"

I dug into the cheap Halloween fabric like I was a dog in search of a buried bone until I came into contact with the first glint of shiny metal.

I paused, stroking the smooth surface with my fingers. My chest ached and constricted like I was anticipating something terrifying or exciting.

Tears fell down my face as I lifted the box from the container I had placed it in less than a month ago. "Why won't you just...stop?" I whispered as I brought the box to my chest and sat down on the floor of my closet. One of the corners dug into my skin and I didn't care. "You leave me and then you do shit like this?" I mumbled. "I liked you better before."

I had no idea if what I was saying even made sense. Nothing else did, so why should it matter?

Realizing that there wasn't going to be an answer, I took the box from my chest and set it on the floor in front of me. I stared at it, still feeling the same pull toward it I had felt since I hid it away. I wanted to set it back on my shelf, open the drawer and offer it some small trinkets, open the lid and find black feathers sitting inside the soft interior. When I rested my hand on top of the lid, I expected there to be some kind of cataclysmic moment. A strong gust of wind, more flies, more fire, knocking and feathers and most importantly, the voice. The voice would come back and talk to me. Tell me things I didn't understand but oddly enough, comfort me and make me feel safe. I needed that right now more than anything. I wanted to be wrapped in the smell of autumn and whispered to as I fell asleep. Anything but these ambiguous moments.

But when I opened the box, nothing but the plain red insides stared back at me. I did not hear or see anything but the emptiness of the box, the closet, my room, and my house. How could something that had consumed so much of my life be so hollow?

I felt like I was stood up on a date or left at the altar. Like I was lost on an island and promised rescue that never came.

Sniffing, I dried the rest of my tears, picked up the box, and stumbled out of my closet. I cleared off my nightstand of my phone, any books, and the small lamp that sat there. This would be the box's place now.

Then I gathered all of the canvases and threw them in the trash. As an afterthought, I uncovered the small black feather from my pillow and placed it back into the box. It wasn't much, but it bothered me how empty it was. I hoped it was enough.

*"Deep into that darkness peering,
long I stood there wondering, fearing..."*

—EDGAR ALLAN POE, *THE RAVEN*

PART THREE:
BIRTH

CHAPTER
TWENTY

IT WAS NOW NEARING SEPTEMBER and most of my life was simultaneously coming together and falling apart. On the outside, Mom had begun cleaning more, getting dressed on a regular basis, and was even thinking about getting a part-time job. On the outside, I was getting ready to start a new semester at school, getting excited for all the courses I would take, working on the weekends and making art with Jordan whenever I could. Although I was still mostly going through my "Boring" period every once in a while I could bang out a realistic portrait or some geometric pattern that actually looked like I tried.

There was a new color I loved, and it technically wasn't a color at all. Black. I drew in the heaviest charcoal and painted with only one tube. I used it to line my eyes, to clothe my skin. I thought about dyeing all of the pink satin in my room the same color, but something stopped me. It was one part of my childhood—my innocent mind—that I could keep. One reminder I didn't lose or question. Of course I always loved black. I was an art major. Of course I loved dark drama. And it wasn't like I had made a drastic change to my wardrobe or had to make any great leaps in the makeup department either. I couldn't figure out what it was, but I wanted to be coated in it. Swathed in the color like I was bathing in ink. I had no interest in other hues, no desire to paint a sunset or a bowl of bruised fruit.

Doctor Howard and I had parted ways. He said I had shown great improvement and was more or less a stable human being. He told me to take it easy and if I ever got too stressed again, I could always come back to talk.

Of course, that was only because he didn't know the truth.

Although the voice hadn't returned, I was hallucinating more these days. What had begun as a spider or fly here or there had grown into larger, more disturbing images. I woke up one morning to find slithering black snakes in my bed, their cool scales rubbing against my bare skin, their small, powerful muscles combing over me like I was merely part of their landscape. For a moment, I thought I was still dreaming, despite the fact that I hadn't had a dream since I was put on medication.

When I jumped up to shake them off and take in the entirety of the situation, nothing stared back at me besides my pink sheets, crinkled and bunched at the end of the bed. But when I lifted my pillow off the floor, there was a single black feather underneath.

It was small, but it meant something.

The box had become more of me. That was the only way to

explain it. I always wanted it near. I even carried it with me in my bag when I went to Jordan's or let it sit in the passenger seat when I went grocery shopping. Anxiety gripped my chest and my hands shook when I couldn't bring it with me—like if I had to take a shower or eat. My hair was dirty and I was losing weight. At first, it scared me how dependent I was on the box's presence. Now, it scared me when I was alone. I was never truly alone with it by my side.

On one of the last weekends before the semester started back up again, Jordan and I set up our supplies outside. I had tucked the box behind a planter before she came over, and I couldn't help staring past her when she talked. Mom wasn't home, and our yard was secluded from any prying eyes, so we took turns posing in our bikinis as we soaked up the last of the summer sun in my overgrown garden. Since my work had taken a turn for crap lately, I preferred posing these days. I could still be a part of the art without the pressure that came with creating it from scratch. It was my idea to ditch the stool and kneel in the dirt. It was my idea to pull the weeds from around me so they covered my bottom half. It was my idea that I should bury my hands in the earth until I couldn't see them anymore.

"You know," Jordan said, peering over her sunglasses and around her easel. "You should model way more. You have this intuition about what'll look good."

I could barely hear her. My pulse pounded in my ears. My heart hammered in my chest. My fingers crushed the dirt into my palms, and when I glanced down I could see and feel black worms wriggling against my skin. I knew they weren't real by now so I didn't even flinch. Actually, I had become excited at the idea of finding more phantoms. It meant that Six—whoever or whatever he was—was here. I didn't know how I knew this, but it was true. Truer than anything I saw or felt. Truer than the drugs that were supposed to stop me from seeing these things. Truer than the lies I told my doctor and my mother.

"You think so?" I asked finally, realizing that more time had passed between us talking than I had intended.

Jordan ran a hand through her even shorter hair. She had shaved the sides a few weeks ago and now they were growing in. "Hell yeah," she said as she took a sip of her spiked lemonade. "I don't know what's gotten into you, but I like it."

I swallowed hard as I stared down at my hands just as the ten minute timer went off. There were no worms now, but I could feel them as if they had fused to the bones of my fingers.

What had gotten into me and how? I wish I knew.

DESPITE MY DESPERATE PLEAS AND adamant foot stomping, Jordan insisted on another party. We were supposed to give summer the "proper send off" and staying sober in any way was out of the question. Before I even got to her house I decided not to drink. Last time was enough for a lifetime of parties. I didn't even bother dressing nicely. I just wore the same paint stained dark jeans and a ripped black t-shirt with the sleeves cut off. I threw my hair into a messy bun and other than making sure there was no eyeliner under my eyes to make my dark circles look deeper, I didn't fuss with makeup either.

"Come on, Corbin!" Jordan yelled from outside my door. "I'm going to be late to my own party."

The box sat on my nightstand, the dark wood shining back at me. I wanted to take it with me, but I was afraid someone would steal it. I didn't know what kind of crazy artsy types would show up. I wasn't even bringing my wallet. With a heavy sigh, I placed my hand on the lid in some silent gesture. I felt almost like apologizing, but I knew better. I had to turn away before I changed my mind, so I turned off the light and opened the door, leaving the box behind.

Jordan was standing in the hall, one foot propped on the wall and her arms crossed over her chest. "You're going like that?" she asked, but she was only half serious. She hadn't changed either, but she had let down the longer side of her hair (it was previously held up by a pencil) and she had also slapped on some dark red lipstick that looked almost purple.

"Like I need to change to play beer pong and sit in your basement," I replied.

Jordan only shrugged. "Just saying. I got that stripper pole installed last week and you won't make many tips looking like that."

I snorted in response as we walked out of my house and to her car.

We got to her house around nine and it was no surprise that everyone was late. College kids—especially art college kids—worked only on their own internal clocks. Jordan's parents were cool. Even if they weren't on vacation somewhere in the Netherlands, they would have probably let her have one of her basement parties as long as no one got alcohol poisoning or pregnant.

We made our way down the stairs to Jordan's underground lair. This was the place she had made into part studio, part living space. Her room was only where she slept. She couldn't hang out in there and she couldn't sleep anywhere else. Once, she told me it had something to do with something that happened in her childhood, but she wouldn't go further than that. She didn't have to. We both had skeletons we'd rather not look at and I was fine with her keeping hers tightly locked up if she was fine with me doing the same. That's why we worked so well. We both had shit happening inside of us that was always coming out at the worst times. Sometimes you needed someone to look at the ugly oil spill near your feet and act like it wasn't there. Sometimes you needed someone to sit with you when the building was on fire.

I took a seat at the bar they had installed and turned myself slowly on one of the swivel chairs. Jordan poured me a rum and coke but I pushed it over to her.

She shrugged and took the drink for herself as she gestured around the room. "So?" she asked. "How'd I do?"

Taking in the large open space, I recognized the usual furniture: the beat up patchwork couch against the wall, the yard sale find bean bag chairs, the TV, the stereo, the long table with cups set up on it all ready for drinking games. There were mismatched Christmas lights strung from the ceiling. Some multicolored, some white, and some in the shapes of chili peppers, flamingos, and even some purple spiders.

"Looks nice," I said with a smile I couldn't really feel. My hands were beginning to shake so I sat on them. "You know what?" I said. "Maybe I will have that drink."

I CAME TO FIND OUT that the lights were mainly because Jordan's plan was to turn on a few black lights and bust out some glow-in-the-dark paint. The light up flamingos and chili peppers were merely just so no one tripped over anyone else. I wasn't a big party person; I mostly just liked watching things unfold. I took a spot on the musty old couch and watched as Jordan and her art friends—some I knew and most I didn't—took green, yellow, and pink black light paint and splattered it all over canvases and each other. Some other people took the initiative to paint the bottoms of their clear beer pong cups with the paint, making the liquid inside look radio-active as the bounced the ball back and forth. The music was loud, too. Something that sounded like jazz by the way the trumpets and saxophones kept blowing, but it was decidedly awful and making my head spin. Or maybe it was the alcohol. Or the ever constant beating in my head and limbs.

The music droned on. My heart slammed against my ribs in an almost painful motion, as if it was fighting me. As if I was the enemy trying to keep it against its will. I wished I had stayed home. I could have sat by myself with my box next to me on my nightstand and watched a movie. I could have fallen asleep with the hopes of burned leaves in my nostrils and feathers in my hands when I woke up.

Instead I was here, getting shit faced when I said I wouldn't, mixing alcohol with my meds when I shouldn't. Being around people when I hated all of them and their over inflated egos. I hated how they called themselves artists and performers when they did little else besides slap some clay into a kiln or walk on stage to do an interpretive dance once in a while.

Anger flared hot in my stomach, and I wasn't even sure why. What exactly was I angry about? Being out of my house and with my friend? A chance to unwind before yet another semester started?

The couch next to me dipped in on one side a little too fast, making my beer slosh over the edge of my clear cup and spill onto my pants. That was all I needed to turn the anger into a flame.

Sighing heavily, I turned to the person next to me. "Do you mind?" I spat, having to adjust my vision because of the darkness and blurred images.

Chess was sitting there, looking as douchey as ever. He was wearing dark pants that were cut into shorts, the edges so frayed he looked like he had run through a potato peeler. He had a multicolored beanie on his head, which only minimally covering his dirty hair, and some tie-dye t-shirt he probably got from the thrift store in an ironic way. A way that said, *ask me about my shirt, I'll tell you I got it from a thrift store.*

"What do you want?" I asked.

He smiled and took my drink from me. "Did you not learn from last time?" he asked.

I expected to become even more pissed off, but instead I found myself staring, watching this scuzz as he smiled like a proud rooster in front of his harem of hens. Like he had his pick of anyone in the room and I should feel important because he was talking to me.

"Okay?" was all I could think of saying. "So, you came over here to annoy me?"

Up until now he had been staring around the room, the ceiling of lights, the people playing games. I was almost an afterthought until he finally turned toward me. He moved in even closer, wrapping his arm around the back of the couch and bringing our faces so close to each other that I could smell...wait. That wasn't alcohol on his breath. It smelled clean. Yet dirty. No, dirt. It smelled like fresh soil. And leaves. Burned leaves and dirt. I looked into his eyes and I could feel it in my hands, the same as I had that afternoon.

"You see?" he asked.

I blinked a few times as my throat and mouth completely dried out. There wasn't enough air in the room and things started getting darker, like each individual miniature bulb had burst.

Chess' face fell. The original confidence and pride had now faded into something more akin to worry. "You aren't happy?"

Words became slush in my mouth that refused to melt. My tongue froze behind my teeth and the room spun out of focus.

Chess gently grabbed my arm. "Let's go outside."

Even if I didn't want to, I doubt I would have had a choice

in the matter. Before I could open my mouth or move away, Chess was ushering me up the basement stairs. I caught Jordan's eye on my way out of the basement and she only raised an eyebrow. She liked that I was with Chess. In her world, we were perfect for each other. Perfect fuck friends for each other, which was all she thought about anyway, so why would I want anything else? God. I was angry again. I couldn't shake it.

Chess grabbed a hold of my hand as soon as we were at the top of the stairs. Good thing, too. My feet felt velcroed to the carpet of Jordan's living room. My skin was hot, and my palm was sweating against the cool softness of his. I didn't remember his skin feeling this way when he was forcing himself onto me. It was like it belonged to someone else entirely.

The crisp night air hit my face and cooled me down for a moment. I couldn't figure out why I was so angry. Why when I saw the flowerbeds in front of Jordan's house that I wanted to tear them out of the dirt and feel them flatten under my boots. Why when I spotted a rusted Buick parked in the driveway that I wanted to smash in the windows.

"It is alright, little crow," the voice said. Only it wasn't the voice. It was Chess'.

It took me what seemed like the longest time to turn around and look at where our hands were clasped together. When I finally did, I saw that the fingers laced through mine were not completely solid. They were made from thick motes of dust, black at the tips and fading into pale skin. My gaze traveled upward, past a broad shoulder covered in a hideous tie-dye t-shirt. I didn't remember that either. Chess was one of those lanky, string bean types. This shirt looked too tight on him. Like he had grown three sizes between the time he had put it on and now.

I swallowed hard, barely noticing that all the anger I had felt only moments ago was gone. I wasn't even buzzed anymore. Everything felt completely and undeniably real.

The same face I saw in my shower. The same one I drew in my sketch book.

"Six," I whispered, unlatching my hand and covering my mouth with it.

The smile he gave me was almost too much to bear. "You say my name naturally now," he said. His voice was the same one I heard at night, the same one I heard in my head. Only this was more than a whisper. Deeper, heavier. There was a weight to it I didn't understand.

My breath came in and out too fast as he grabbed my hand again and led me to the side of the house, a small space between Jordan's home and her neighbors'. He positioned me against the bricks of the protruding chimney and took half a step back. I noticed that the longer he was in front of me, the more the flimsy film of black dust covered his hands, traveled up his arms.

"I don't understand," I whispered.

He stared down at my hand still in his, though I couldn't even feel it there anymore. It was like I was merely clenching my fist. He released me and I wrapped my arms around myself to keep from falling over. I was grateful for the bricks behind me.

"There isn't much time," he said. "I can only appear as

this...man...for so long."

I stared into his black eyes—eyes that also did not belong to Chess. "What do you want?"

He closed the distance between us and I pressed myself into the wall more. I wasn't afraid of him; I was afraid of what he meant. Of whether I was really seeing him or if I was dreaming with my eyes completely open. Maybe someone slipped some Molly into my drink or something. Art kids are all about that shit.

"I need...more," he said in a low voice close to my face. I could feel his cool breath against my cheeks, rustling my hair. He moved his arms to his sides so I could no longer see them. Or maybe they were disappearing. I couldn't tell.

"More what?" I asked.

He hesitated, then gently grazed his nose against my cheek. I felt the same pins and needles against my skin as when he kissed me in the dark, the same speeding of my pulse and thoughts crashing against my body and mind. "More of you."

The words redirected the pins and needles right to my spine and up the back of my head. "I don't..." But I couldn't finish the sentence. The words got stuck in my throat and wouldn't budge any further.

"Energy," he said. "More fire. More...you."

"Fire?" I echoed weakly. Had he somehow made me angry so he could use it as fuel to appear?

The realization must have shown on my face because he said, "Yessss," his voice turning into more of the whisper I was used to.

I searched his face. The strong jaw, the gently sloping nose. "Why?" was the only thing I could say.

A small smile appeared on his full lips. "Always questions. Always expecting answers she already knows."

And I did know. Somewhere, deep down, I knew that if this wasn't in my head, if this was as real as he told me, energy made him real. Made him appear in front of me. Made me less insane.

"How?" I asked, finally finding the normal volume of my voice. "How do I help?"

His smile broadened. He was probably expecting this to be harder. More arguing. More questions. But I was tired of questions. I was tired of fighting with myself. If this was what it took to finally be at peace, so be it.

"The box," he said simply. "Sleep with it open."

"What will that do?"

He stared down at his shoulder, the t-shirt turning black in the dim light, disappearing along with his skin into more ash. "I will show you," he said. I felt something touch my face, but there was no hand to speak of. Just the gentle caress of something that wasn't there. "Then I will become...more."

I thought of the canvases in my room. The flies that no one seemed to remember but me. "No fire. No bugs."

A small, soft laugh escaped him now. "As you wish."

That was all either of us said for the longest time. We just stood there, staring at one another, taking in every detail. When I glanced past his shoulders, down his stomach and to the band of his jeans, there was nothing there but darkness. It was like he was a photograph only partially developed.

"I only want you," he whispered, breaking my concentration and redirecting my eyes back to his. "I only want..."

"More," I finished for him.

A sad smile formed on his mouth now, and he nodded once.

"Why me?" I asked. "Why am I the one to help you?"

He looked into my eyes. "More questions," was all he said, as if that was enough of an answer. "Close your eyes."

My heart sped up again and my face became hot, but this time I wasn't mad. A surprising calm washed over me instead. I closed my eyes. I figured he didn't want me to watch him disappear, and that was fine with me. Especially when I thought about the bathroom of Cedar Ridge.

When he spoke again, his voice came from right in front of my face. "My little crow," he cooed. "My lotus in the mud. You have no idea how special you are to me."

My breath caught in my throat as he kissed me. It wasn't the same as I felt in the darkness of my room. This was more solid. I felt it at the back of my skull. The moon pulling the tide in an endless rhythm of give and take.

Then I opened my eyes and he was gone.

CHAPTER
TWENTY
ONE

I GOT IN LATE THAT night. Call me crazy, but I didn't exactly want to go back into the basement and try to chill with a bunch of people I didn't know—especially after what happened outside. Instead of trying to find Jordan in the throngs of art kids, booming music, and glow-in-the-dark paint, I decided it would be best if I walked home. I needed the air.

Jordan only lived a few miles away and if I concentrated on my feet as they carried me, it didn't seem like a long time before I was in front of my house. The lights were all off. Mom was asleep, and I had to fumble with my keys in the dark because the porch light was out. I was tempted to just plop onto my bed and pass out, but I didn't want to look to my left and see the box sitting there on my night table. I didn't want to sleep with it open.

I didn't want to wake up the next morning with it the same as it was right now: empty.

Instead, I went into the bathroom and filled the tub with the hottest water I could get, immediately steaming up the entire room and fogging the mirror over with a faint film. I stripped out of my clothes slowly, half expecting a disembodied torso to appear out of nowhere. But deep down, I knew he wouldn't be visiting for a little while. It must have taken a lot out of him to see me tonight. Just to tell me to sleep with the box open. Yeah, maybe it was in my head after all.

Clearing a spot in the fog of the mirror, I stared at myself for a few long seconds. The mark on my leg was completely gone and hadn't reappeared. But my shoulder and face were smudged in what looked like charcoal. I took a step closer, blinking like it wasn't really there.

Dark black soot covered my right shoulder, like someone with dirty hands had gripped it and was dragged away unexpectedly. I could see four finger marks as plain as my own, whereas my face was a more amorphous blob, reminding me of the paintings I had created only days before.

I stared down at my hand and the entire palm was black. And my face. It looked like I had fallen into a bucket of black paint, splatters of it against my chin and across my lips.

Like I needed more proof, I crouched down and retrieved my clothes from the linoleum. The shoulder of my shirt had an identical mark as well.

Not wanting to think any more tonight, I turned away from

the mirror and stepped into the bath. The water was on the verge of scalding, but I didn't care. It gave me something to focus on other than the surging and swelling thoughts floating around in my mind.

Skin raw and red, black marks scrubbed off, I dressed in shorts and a tank top for bed. I was overheated from my boiling bath and the coolness of my silk sheets was comforting. I turned to my nightstand, looking past the box to retrieve my prescription bottle and bottle of water I kept behind it. I took my sleeping pill and gulped down the water, suddenly feeling exhausted and dehydrated. I threw the empty bottle on the ground, telling myself I would pick it up later when there were countless others already kicked under my bed. Placing the orange prescription bottle back on my nightstand, my hand grazed the smooth surface of the box. I turned out the bedside lamp and picked up the box. Sitting up a little straighter with my back against the headboard, I stared down at the shiny metalwork I could see in the dim glow of the night light. The wood was warm whereas the metal was always cool. It was something I had come to count on. Like the changing of seasons. It was definite. Always varying, but true.

Taking a deep breath, I closed my eyes, completely in awe as to how much I would believe if it meant I wasn't insane. Something out of this world was better than my mind slipping into that same dark place as my mother and my grandmother before her.

I slowly opened the box and stared into the rich warm

interior. Almost immediately, I could smell freshly fallen leaves—not quite dead. Not yet. There were no feathers this time, just the empty red velvet. I placed as much of my hand that would fit into it and felt that it was even warmer than the wood on the outside, like I was reaching into the heart of something and anticipating when it would begin beating.

"No fire and no bugs," I whispered before reluctantly setting the open box on my nightstand. I curled up on my side facing it, placing my head on the pillow, hoping sleep would sink around me before anything happened.

CHAPTER
TWENTY
TWO

HEAVY HEAD AND HEAVY EYES. Weighted limbs. I wasn't able to move in any direction. Just lie there. Something held me, refusing to let me wake fully or fall deeper into sleep.

Colors played behind my eyelids like an oil spill. Green, purple, then blue and yellow—all swirling around each other but never mixing. The shape of something long and bright curled on itself before straightening again. I couldn't decipher what it was. As soon as the name for the image settled on my tongue, it disintegrated, leaving nothing but fragments of the idea.

Shhh.

It was the sound I had been waiting for since I returned home.

I wanted to speak, but my lips would not move. I felt something light and gentle on my hands, reassuring me that everything was okay. I hadn't realized how badly I needed to know that until the warmth spread throughout me, my heartbeat slowed, and I released a deep breath.

That's better.

I found that the less I concentrated, the easier it was to move. My head lolled to one side and then the other. I was able to whisper, but it sounded strange to my ears, like the vibrations of something completely inhuman coming from the back of my throat.

"Six?"

My head slipped to the right, heavier than it had felt before. Something soft touched either sides of my face, stopping the movement.

Yesss. Say it again.

My mouth became dry and I had to swallow several times before I could say anything. There was so much I wanted to say. If this was the reason why I slept with the box open, if this was why he had taken the form of what had to be my least favorite person on earth. But all I could seem to say, all I *wanted* to say, was one word.

"Six." This time it wasn't a question and it came out fuller, more solid.

A short exhalation, a sigh as if a great weight had been lifted from something not meant to carry so much. *That's my love*, he said on a breath.

There was a weight on me that I could not describe. It wasn't exactly heavy, but it was defined. No longer a shadow as it previously had felt.

"Why can't I open my eyes?" I whispered into the pools of colors playing behind my eyelids. They had stopped forming actual shapes and instead just floated past one another lazily.

I do not have the strength to become a different form right now. I do not want you to see.

Thoughts of the night in the bathroom at Cedar Ridge snapped through my mind in quick succession. I recognized all the images, but they flipped past me too quickly to focus on one in particular. "Can I touch you?" I asked, knowing that I was only slightly asking permission. The rest of me was asking if it was *possible*.

Are you ready for that, little crow? he asked, a hint of playfulness in the whisper.

"Not like that." I found it hard to keep a smile off of my lips. "If I can't see you...I need something else. Something that tells me you're real."

There was a pause. Some contemplation or hesitation as to what he should do next. Maybe he had disappeared altogether. *I only have a short time,* he said. *I only came to see how you were.*

"Why?"

I scared you.

My fingers tingled with anticipation. I couldn't take it anymore. 'So can I touch you or not?"

This time he did laugh; just the smallest, lightest whisper of a sound. There was no other response, just the flimsy weight of whatever was holding down my arms loosening. My hands shook before I had even made a decision as to where to put them.

I was getting some of what I wanted, wasn't I? I wasn't able to see him, but at least if he was solid, if he was really here, I could feel him and make up what he looked like—as if I hadn't already.

Raising my arm, I slowly moved my fingers in the air, touching nothing until I came into contact with what felt like cotton. Only it was softer and cooler than any fabric I had felt before. Underneath, there were obvious muscles, but they didn't fit where I thought they should. What should have been a shoulder felt like an arm, what was supposed to be smooth felt rough. And something thin and spindly within the softness emerged. I didn't know what to make of it.

"Where is your face?" I asked, half afraid that he maybe didn't have one.

Up more, my love.

The more I moved, the more I shook. I wasn't cold, but goose bumps formed on my arms and chest. My palm smoothed upward, sliding across cool silkiness—I couldn't exactly call it skin. It didn't feel like flesh at all. Finally, I felt something that resembled a neck. It was rough, but not unpleasant. I didn't linger there long before my hand settled on something that finally felt familiar—real skin, just like mine, only softer.

There, he whispered, all traces of amusement gone.

My heart sped up again as I trailed my fingers lightly across the expanse of his jaw, the ridge of a nose, and then lightly, the tips of eyelashes and brows. I wanted to touch his lips, but this wasn't enough.

"Will you kiss me again?" I asked.

The skin under my fingers stretched in what I hoped was a smile before the realest part of him touched my lips. And it was the realest part. Never before had the kiss I experienced in the dark felt this soft, this warm. The smell of leaves filled my nose as if we were not in my room in my house, but in the woods in the mud. A cool tongue teased mine from my mouth and my breathing picked up as my hand fell away from him, glued back to the spot it had originally been before the kiss broke apart like shattered glass.

Something in me broke as well. I couldn't pin point where the fissure started, but the crack spread over my entire body, making my chest ache and my throat tight. "Please," I practically begged.

I heard something shift nearby; it was between something like pages being turned or blankets shrugged around a body. *What is it, little crow*

I struggled to find the words as my eyes burned behind my lids. I fought with the sheets under my palms, my fingers the only things I could move as they clenched around the fabric.

The voice came closer, inches from my face. *I will give you anything you ask of me,* he cooed. *You only need to say the word.*

"Please stay," I finally whispered. "Don't leave me all alone."

I didn't want the box to snap shut. I didn't want everything to be empty again.

Shhh. It was the sound of an autumn breeze, bringing with it the smell of earth and fire. *I will stay as long as I can in this form,* he said, *but I am always with you. Surely you know that by now.*

The covers around me moved like someone now laid to the side, and I found that a moment later I could roll over, my back pressed against the contrasting smoothness of the skin of his face and the rough, scale-like texture of a chest. Something covered the top part of my body, from torso to head, blocking out whatever dimness the nightlight shone in the dark and making everything an endless pool of black.

CHAPTER
TWENTY
THREE

I WAS ALMOST GRATEFUL FOR the familiar burnt smell without any hint of cinnamon that morning. I didn't think I could deal with that right now. My head pounded and I was sweating so much that I wasn't sure if I had swam in my sleep. Kicking off the remaining blankets, I sat up in bed and rubbed my swollen eyes. I was still unbearably hot and sticky; I wondered if Mom had turned off the air when she woke up. Everything blurred before coming into focus as I blinked. At first I thought all the black I saw was from left over makeup or maybe even hair lingering in my face, but as my brain registered what my eyes were seeing, I could tell that this wasn't the case.

Thousands of black, iridescent feathers covered the sheets beneath my bare legs. I couldn't even see the pink. Fear wasn't the word, but comfort wasn't it either. My trembling hand hovered over the mass of smoothness until finally, I was brave enough to pick one up and hold it between my fingers. They weren't just black, but blue, red, green—all of these colors switched just beneath the surface, playing on the black backdrop. Was this what happened when he left me now? Was this what Six left behind? Not flies or fire, but feathers?

But there was something else that wasn't quite right. Something at the back of my head that tugged gently. I turned to look at my nightstand where the box sat and it was gone, the only thing in its place a smudged charcoal handprint.

I was saddened by the fact that I couldn't hold it, that I couldn't fill it with as many feathers as I could before I cleaned up the rest as if they wouldn't disappear the moment I tried to show anyone. I didn't even get to say goodbye. Then again, it was obvious who took it.

My stomach lurched. What if this was his plan? What if he only wanted the box and not me? What if the feathers were some kind of consolation prize for all my trouble and I would never see him again?

I sat up straighter, staring at the pink canopy above me. When had I accepted that this was real? It was a definite possibility that last night, the box, the smudges were all in my head. That they always were and always would be and obviously whatever medication I took wasn't working or helping, but fueling the hallucinations.

I bolted out of bed and didn't even bother changing out of

my sleep shirt as I made my way into the kitchen. I didn't want to look at my room anymore. I didn't want to wonder if things were real or imaginary.

Mom was nowhere in sight, but I heard the water running in the shower, so I figured she had tried to make breakfast, failed, then decided to wash off the morning. She told me she did that. When things were really bad some small part of her believed she could wash it away like the dirt from her garden.

The toast sat on the counter in one of the only clear spaces, black and bark-like, filling the air with its presence. I picked it up and decided to at least make it look like I ate so when Mom came out of the shower, clean and new, she would feel better. I turned toward the stove and saw a pan with stuck on burnt eggs soaking in the bubbly water of the sink, the carton of eggs still out on the counter.

With a friend.

At first I thought it was just a shadow, just a reflection of one of the many wind chimes casting on the counter near the stove. I immediately wanted to go back to my room, crawl under the covers, and try to forget everything, but then I remembered that was why I had come into the kitchen in the first place.

The carton was open, the brown eggs a stark contrast against the harsh black of the thing with its mouth wrapped around one.

I hadn't realized that I dropped the plate until I heard it crash on the dusty linoleum, the blue ceramic remnants scattering under the fridge and around my bare feet.

A thick, black snake was half curled around the cardboard of the egg container, its neck stretched forward, eyes staring straight ahead as its jaw unlatched and it tried to swallow the egg whole.

The same ache in my chest from last night fluttered beneath the surface as I watched, my pulse racing, as the reptile became one with its avian neighbor.

I didn't exactly know what to do. If this was real, snakes could be poisonous. Or constrict. But we didn't exactly live in a place where snakes snuck into the house and raided our kitchens for snacks.

If this wasn't real...I had a whole new set of problems to deal with.

But I couldn't just stand there between the two options and all the outcomes that trailed behind them. I had to do something. I couldn't just wait and see anymore. I knew Mom had a ton of things I could use to get the snake out of the house; I just had to find one. I inched backwards toward the table, reaching behind me and shuffling through papers, junk mail and probably a few bills before landing on something solid. When I withdrew my hand, I discovered my fingers were wrapped around the handle of a cooking pot. Perfect.

I approached the little guy carefully, unsure if I was afraid of it or just trying to save it—from what, I wasn't sure. I expected it to slither away as soon as it saw me coming, but it only shifted its narrowed black eyes, its mouth still firmly around the egg. Positioning the pot just under the edge of the carton, I took a deep breath, and as I slid next to the counter, I took a wooden spoon from the nearby drawer and began sliding it in. It didn't even budge. It just continued to stare, repositioning its jaw every so often to engulf more of its prey. I finally got the creature into the pot, egg included. Thankfully, it was preoccupied and didn't really pay me much attention.

Stepping quickly and carefully, I shuffled over to the back door, outside and into the backyard. I placed the pot on the ground and tipped it slightly near the edge of Mom's dilapidated garden, convincing myself that it was far enough; I didn't want the snake to suddenly wise up and strike at me for moving it.

I let out another breath as I stood from my semi-crouched position. When I turned back, the snake was still there, crawling out of the pot and resting in the dead grass, it's blue-black scales glinting in the morning sun. So far, it was all real. Weird, but real.

Suddenly, the heat I felt in my room had returned. At first I thought it was the sun in the early morning, but I hadn't felt it when I walked outside. It was so urgent and so strong that it sucked the moisture from my skin, made my mouth dry and my vision blur. Before I knew what was happening, I was on the ground, sprawled in the dirt, and I couldn't really move too well. I jerked forward, as if some unseen force had swiped at my ankles and brought my feet out from under me. My lungs filled with the smell of smoke so strong that it choked me and I couldn't breathe. Hands on the ground and crawling on all fours, I tried to keep upright so I wouldn't collapse on top of the snake in front of me. Bursts of multicolored light sparkled in my vision like confetti at a sad birthday party before everything tunneled and I retched uncontrollably. It felt like I would never fully catch my breath as everything turned black. But what slipped out of my mouth was worse.

When I could see again and looked forward to where the snake still sat, the egg nearly completely consumed, there were three more. I had no idea where they had come from, but they were coiling around the first, making it look larger than it was. The first one stared directly at me with its little black eyes, daring me to question its existence. My mouth was wet and tasted sour. When I wiped it with a shaking hand expecting vomit, all that was smeared on my fingers was black ink. Beneath me, another snake was uncoiling near my feet, its black scales shining in the hot sun as it smoothly joined the rest.

"What the hell?" I whispered.

I wasn't expecting an answer. "Corbin, just try and relax. We're trying to help you."

I turned my head from left to right, the snakes, trees, dirt and sunlight smearing into one vague color. There was no one there but me.

"Oh, sweetheart."

It was my Mom's voice, and she sounded like she was crying.

Another wave of heat slammed into me, knocking me further into the ground. This time when I looked to my arms that would not move, someone was there with me.

I didn't recognize him. His dark hair, glasses, and clean polo shirt as he leaned over me, keeping a hold of my wrist. My mother was attached to the other, holding firmly so I couldn't get away or sit up.

A small amount of blood trickled from the bend in my left elbow, and an empty syringe lay not far from us.

"What the fuck is going on?" It came out sounding more desperate than I intended and I struggled against them.

"It's okay," Mom said into my ear as everything spun around me. "The doctor is going to help you, sweetie. Don't worry."

I tried to stare at her to ask what she meant, but she swirled and became liquid. When I turned my head to the right, the "doctor" was taking another syringe out of his back pocket and he didn't even hesitate before plunging it into my right arm. Whatever this one was, it was considerably stronger than anything I'd ever been given. My eyes rolled back in my head, my stomach dropped, and my body went limp.

"That's it," said the man I didn't know. "We'll get her to the hospital and figure this out. Don't worry."

I heard Mom sob as she lifted my head into her lap. "I've never seen her like that," she said. "She completely ignored me. It was like I wasn't even there and then she was in the dirt, digging. I thought she was trying to bury herself."

My mind spun as Mom continued to cry over me. I managed to focus my vision enough to see the hole I must have dug. It looked like a hole that took more time to dig than the three minutes I had stepped outside. It was just next to Mom's weed-choked vegetable patch. It was so deep that I couldn't see the bottom and a mound of dirt lay next to the pot, sans snakes.

My eyes closed again, too dry to concentrate on anything else. A few tears squeezed out between my lashes as the world went dark around me. I was terrified of where I might wake up and what was real. If that would change when I came out on the other side of the darkness.

But through the fog, I heard the voice, full and solid and in my ear as someone lifted me in their arms.

"I've got you, my love. I've got you."

CHAPTER

TWENTY
FOUR

THERE ARE SO MANY THINGS that hide in the dark. Things that bump and bite, nothing but clumsy teeth trying to move forward. Then there are things like me; things that crawl and slither and flutter towards something. The box was only a temporary vessel. Somewhere I could wait patiently. Somewhere I could exist in the smallest of ways.

Then there was the little crow.

I had known her in many lifetimes. She had been many people and many beings, but none were as alluring as this. None had made it possible to interact. Her mind was a labyrinth of sorts, every turn something new to overcome or convince.

Oftentimes, belief is only conjured when there is nothing left to choose. They raise their temples and praise their gods; they pray for their sick. They believe. They believe because they need to. Because they are afraid of what their lives would mean if they had no beliefs.

All I needed to come forth was this fleeting emotion. Just one person to believe. And I had found her. I had loved her. She was my beginning and end. My mother, sibling, lover. She was me and her. She was everything human and inhuman—the crow and the tree.

My lost and my love.

The minute she opened the box, she became my door into this world.

CHAPTER
TWENTY
FIVE

I COULD FEEL SOMETHING SOFT. A blanket, maybe.

Then my hands. My hands were tingling with lack of circulation and I remembered the world I had left behind before the darkness took me. I was probably strapped to a hospital gurney and I wasn't ready to face that. But against my will, my eyes bolted open and I only saw a blur of colors. I had to blink a few times before anything became solid and stayed still, and even then, the images shifted and swayed like they were made out of liquid.

I wasn't in a hospital. Instead of the stark, bright whiteness I was expecting, I was greeted by dark walls, dark leather furniture, and deep cherry wood floors. The only thing that wasn't black was one wall, where it looked like whoever decorated had forgotten to paint over the white wall midway and all that showed evidence of the fact was a few smudges of a first coat of black paint that matched the rest of the room.

Slowly, I inched myself backward until my back bent, until I was somewhat in a sitting position. A black silk blanket slouched down and pooled in my lap as I reached up my bound wrists so I could rub at my tired eyes. Something heavy clattered to the floor, but I was too distracted to see what it was.

"You're awake."

The sudden noise made me jump and my heart leapt onto my tongue, threatening to spew forth from my mouth. Before I could turn my head, I saw two lean legs dressed in dark pants come into view. When my eyes shifted upward, I saw a black shirt outlined in a suit jacket of the exact same shade. A light blue tie under the collar. I couldn't make myself look up more than that. My eyes shot back down to the floor.

The two dark legs bent at the knee and he sat on the coffee table in front of me.

"Who are you?" I asked.

He picked up what I had dropped and set it on the coffee table. I shouldn't have been surprised the box was here. It was the cause of all of it, after all. The dark eyes blinked at me, the full lips smiled slightly, pulling at one corner of the mouth. "You know."

I stared down at my hands, bound in my lap with some silky material. The skin itself was caked with dried mud and bloody scrapes and scratches. My face felt dirty too. "No," I said nervously. "But if you're looking for money, I don't have any." I heard how shrill and panicked my voice was becoming, and I tried to keep it steady by speaking more. "Although…" I laughed, shaking my head. I refused to look up at the face in front of me again. It was too much. "You're in for a real treat when you try to withdraw from my bank account," I said. "Do you really need a hundred dollars that badly? Because I'd like to avoid the overdraft fees."

He was suddenly closer, his face inches from mine as if he was searching for something that I couldn't see. I still didn't look. Instead, I let him hover near my temple. "Hush," he said, placing a gentle hand on my shoulder and guiding me back onto the couch so I was lying down once more. "Rest," he said.

My head was spinning and I could still feel the sedative on the back of my tongue, the heaviness of my limbs.

This was a hallucination. Granted, my most vivid one yet, but still a hallucination. Boy, would the doctors be happy when they found out what they had done. Instead of making the voices go away, they had brought them forth in the flesh. I laughed quietly to myself. This wasn't real. None of this was real. It was only another figment of my imagination, and if I had full control of my mind, I could wave a hand over the image of this man and dissolve him into nothing.

"Hush," he said again. "They gave you something very strong, my love. You need to rest."

I shook my head. "I need a straight jacket," I mumbled. I wasn't sure if any of the words actually left my mouth in an order that anyone would be able to understand. "Not real," I mumbled. "All in my head."

"Shhhh." The blanket was drawn back over me and tucked around my shoulders. I knew I was hallucinating now. The hospital blankets were always scratchy and too thin. This one was full and soft as it grazed my chin. "We can talk later, little crow," he said.

I knew in the back of my mind who was talking to me, touching me, smiling with the human face and studying me with the human eyes. If I said it or even thought it, I was giving the fantasy power. I was only fueling the hallucinations. If I wanted to get out of here, I needed to ignore it, not give it any more attention than a fly.

I felt the couch dip in next to me. My hair was moved from my face. "I have you, my love," he said, his voice deep and reassuring. It was the sound of rain in the parched desert, the sound of all the creatures that had waited until the earth was damp until they emerged from their dark, hidden spaces. "Rest. I have you now."

TO BE CONTINUED...

ACKNOWLEDGEMENTS

I would like to thank everyone for sticking with me on my writing journey. I find myself and lose myself with every book, and it is them who always make sure I come back more or less in one piece. Amanda, you are the best editor a girl could want. My workshop friends Alec, Kim, Marissa, Brielle, and Sarah; you guys always know just what I need to push my stories over the edge. I can only hope I do the same for you sometimes. Al, thank you for being my first ever reader for this one and drawing me little pictures of cheese when things sounded cheesy.

Thanks to my Nikki Rae Fan Group on Facebook for being my cheerleaders and friends, and thank you to any reader who gives my words a chance.

ABOUT NIKKI

Nikki Rae is an independent author and editor who lives in New Jersey. She explores human nature through fiction, concentrating on making the imaginary as real as possible. Her genres of choice are mainly dark, scary, romantic tales, but she'll try anything once. When she is not writing, reading, or thinking, you can find her spending time with animals, drawing in a quiet corner, or studying people. Closely.

Made in the USA
Middletown, DE
01 June 2016